DARK BEGINNINGS

A LANCE BRODY NOVELLA (BOOK 0)

MICHAEL ROBERTSON, JR.

ISBN: 9781520326962

AUTHOR'S NOTE

DARK BEGINNINGS is a 100-page prequel novella and the true beginning of the Lance Brody series – whose first novel is DARK GAME and is available now. This novella will answer additional questions you may have about Lance and his journey, and also explore a bit of his past, where he came from ... and who he's running from. I hope you enjoy!

-Michael Robertson Jr

1993

Pamela Brody was a lot of things.

Pretty? Absolutely, in that girl-next-door sort of way.

Funny? Hell, she was downright knee-slap hysterical when she got going. Witty and quick as lightning.

Smart? Name a book and she'd probably read it. She had the start of a small library piled in stacks around her home. Everything from Freud to Stephen King to a biography of Benjamin Franklin.

Odd? Well, yes, that word did get tossed around in conversations in which her name would come up. Not so much in a negative light, but in a *we can't really figure her out* way. The fact that no serious boyfriends had managed to stick around longer than a month or two only fueled the small town's gossip fires further in this regard. Who was she, really?

The list of adjectives was immense and varied.

But the adjective that would best describe twenty-four-year-old Pamela Brody on the night of April 13, 1993, was *aroused*.

Which *was* odd. Since on that night, at just a few minutes past eleven o'clock, Pamela Brody was scaling the fence of the

Great Hillston Cemetery. Yes, that was actually its name, as if there were anything great about death.

———

Pamela swung one leg over the top of the wrought-iron rails, then the other, her flowered cotton sundress catching momentarily on one of the rods before she pulled it clear and let herself fall the five or six feet to the ground. Her dress puffed out around her like in that scene from the *Alice in Wonderland* cartoon, and then her bare feet hit the grass and she bent her knees and rolled once before popping back up quickly and saying, "See? Easiest thing in the world."

From the other side of the fence, staring at her and clearly trying to figure out what he'd gotten himself into, the young man in the tweed jacket who'd stopped in town yesterday for a week's worth of business said, "I never said it wasn't easy. I suggested it wasn't the best idea. We're trespassing, and ... well..." He shrugged, nodding toward the scene behind Pamela. "You have to admit it's a bit creepy."

She smiled at him coyly, turned her head just slightly and said, "I didn't take you for the type to be afraid of ghosts."

They'd met last night at the local sports bar. He'd stopped in because it was the first place he'd found to get something to eat that was close to his motel, and she'd been there to watch the Chicago Bulls match-up against their Eastern Conference rival, Detroit. He'd noticed her right away; the way she sat alone, seemingly oblivious to the crowds around her, the simple way she was dressed—in a sundress similar to the one she wore tonight, only the slightest hint of makeup on her face. She appeared completely and at ease with herself and her surroundings. She appeared so *neutral*. A few folks stopped and spoke to her, each one greeted with a smile and some polite conversation, but her attention always turned quickly back to the game, especially when MJ had the ball.

"I'm not afraid of ghosts." Even as he said the words, he didn't believe them himself. And honestly, one didn't often question oneself about the existence of ghosts. It wasn't something most people held serious debates about on a whim—or on a *date*. But it was amazing how quickly the plausibility of the spirit world came into view when one stood mere feet away from one of the oldest and largest cemeteries in the state, and with the hour quickly approaching midnight. He looked up to the sky, just as a strong gust of wind blew through, rattling the iron fencing and whistling through tree limbs. A black cloud rolled across the moon, a cancerous spot growing across the surface. The man ran a hand through his blond hair, sighed. "I think it might storm."

Pamela turned and walked away, toward the tombstones and mausoleums. Another breeze blew and kicked her dress up around her thighs. She made no effort at modesty, just shouted back over her shoulder, "So now you're afraid of getting wet, too?"

At halftime he'd gone over and sat on the stool next to her, offered to buy her another drink. She turned and looked at him and when her eyes met his, he was filled with something he could only describe as being dunked into a perfectly warm bath. She smiled, and his world lit up, his head reeling with the strange mixture of love and sensuality and desire this girl seemed to put out ... radiate. She accepted the drink—an iced tea, which he found cutely conservative—and they introduced themselves and they talked about the game and what he did for work and what there was to do in such a small town, and with two minutes left in the game he asked if he could take her to dinner tomorrow night. She had smiled, accepted, and then kissed him on the cheek before standing and leaving the bar.

Leaving him alone on the stool and wondering who this girl was he'd just met.

After the flash of Pamela's bare thighs, the man cursed under his breath and then heaved himself up and over the fence. His loafers slipped on the railing, but, tall as he was—a good bit over six feet—the effort needed was minimal. He landed softly on the other side and found that he'd started to sweat despite the cool spring night. He took off his jacket, folded it over his arm and hurried off after Pamela.

She was walking through the rows of headstones, periodically stopping and kneeling down to examine the names and dates and epitaphs. Sometimes she would reach out and rest her hand on the marker, a gentle gesture of sympathy. Sometimes she would shake her head slowly, as if digesting terrible news. Sometimes she would grin and stand and act like she'd just heard a dirty joke.

The man watched her silently for a while, then came up behind her and said, "Do you do this often?"

She turned and took his hand and led him away with her, deeper among the graves. "People are always so sad about death," she said, running her fingers across the top of another stone. "They bring so much negative energy into these places. I wish more of them would stop and appreciate the beauty around them."

"Beauty?" he asked.

She stopped and let go of his hand, holding her palms up and gesturing at all around her. "Look around. Look at all these tributes to lives lived, all these markers of memories. Entire generations of people lie here. Histories." She raised a hand to her ear. "Listen," she said.

Another gust of wind blew through the trees, screamed through gaps in mausoleum walls. Then silence.

The man shivered. "What am I hearing?"

4

She looked up at him and smiled. "Peace," she said. "The voices of the resting."

A light sprinkle of rain began to fall, tiny droplets of water peppering Pamela's forehead, as if she glistened with sweat.

The man grew irritated as the cold rain increased and his shirt stuck to him, his hair matting to his head.

Only the sight of Pamela's nipples stiffening beneath her dress kept him in place, made him ask, "Pam, why are we here? Why did you bring me here?"

She went up onto her tiptoes and kissed him on the mouth, rainwater dripping down both their faces. When she pulled away: "Because I like you. And this is one of my favorite places. I wanted to share it with you."

A crack of thunder shouted in the distance. Not on top of them, but closer than the man would have liked. He glanced back the way they'd come, back up the pathway between the headstones. Through the fencing he could still barely make out the darkened shadow that was his car, parked along the back-road they'd taken. So close, yet it seemed so far. Something urged him to go back, to get in that car and drive away. Away from Pamela and away from Hillston. Work be damned.

He shivered, wiped water from his eyes, and then turned back to Pamela. When he saw her, when he met her eyes, that warm-bath feeling hit him again. He let his gaze soak her in, his eyes slowly rolling down her body, admiring the way the wet fabric clung to her and showed off her slender figure. He felt a stirring down below, and just as quickly as the thought had occurred to him, the idea of the car and running away fled from memory.

Pamela said nothing. She took his hand and pulled him deeper into the cemetery. He allowed her to lead him, following a twisting path of gravel around a small bend. When they made it around the corner, Pamela pulled him left, into the grass. His loafers squished and squashed through the soggy ground, and if he'd not been overcome by the allure of the woman before him, he would have cursed at the thought of having to purchase a new pair.

Another crack of thunder boomed, this time much closer. Too close. The rain kicked up another notch, and soon the sound of the falling droplets drowned out all other sound. The clouds rolled in heavier, completely engulfing the moon. Darkness seeped in. He could only see a few feet in front of him now, enough to make out Pamela's slim shoulders.

A few yards ahead a large oak tree, one that looked as though it had begun its life well before the first person was laid to rest in the Great Hillston Cemetery, sprawled up and out of the earth. It towered toward the sky, its limbs forming a near-perfect umbrella from the rain. Pamela pulled him under the cover, and then the two of them stood there together, hands still intertwined, and watched and listened to the onslaught of weather.

Then a bolt of lightning sliced through the sky and the man was again hit with the urge to run. He turned to protest their misadventure, but Pamela had pulled away and was peeling off her dress. Even in the near-darkness he could make out the fine curves of her body, his eyes lingering at her chest, small but firm and perfect. Her wet hair fell around her face, dripped onto her shoulders. Her intentions were clear.

The man tossed his jacket onto the ground under their canopy of branches and fervently undressed. She smiled as he struggled with his pants, hopping from foot to foot like a clumsy fool.

But then he was with her, laying her down atop his jacket—another new purchase that would need to be made—and feeling the surprising warmth of her skin. They kissed, hungrily, and any concern the man had had before vanished as quickly as

Pamela's dress had. She guided him inside her, the warmth of her nearly melting him, his arms and shoulders shuddering. For the next few minutes, the entire rest of the world evaporated, and the man marveled at how he could ever have been so stupid to want to turn away from what would end up being the most erotic moment of his life. He knew he wouldn't be able to continue much longer; he was getting close.

And then the lightning streaked the sky and crashed to the ground what felt like mere feet from where Pamela and the man were lying. And when it did, two things happened.

First, the man let out a small groan of pleasure as he finished, spilling himself inside her and nearly falling forward on arms of jelly.

Second, when the lightning crashed down, electrifying the air around them and seemingly rattling their bones, the darkness had lit up in a brilliant flash of white and gold, a single pulse from a great strobe light. A freeze frame in the night.

And the man had screamed.

Not because he was startled by the noise and the light, but because when the great spotlight had flashed on them, the man had seen the faces of what had to be at least a hundred people all around them, a close circle of spectators all huddled together and watching with great interest.

Just a blip, a quick snapshot that would be forever etched in his memory. But he knew exactly who they were, as well as he knew his own name.

The spirits of the Great Hillston Cemetery had come out for a show that night.

And they'd been smiling.

After he'd screamed, the man struggled to untangle himself from Pamela, slipping on the wet earth and scrambling after his clothes. He didn't offer any parting words, no explanation. Fear had seized him, a puppet master, and he the puppet. He shoved himself into his pants, putting them on backward, grabbed his shirt and left his shoes and jacket behind. And then he was running, back down the path, back to his car.

Pamela Brody watched him go, never once even calling out after him. Simply stunned at what had just unfolded before her. After a while, she laid her head back and closed her eyes, listening to the sounds of the storm around her, feeling surprisingly at peace.

She would never see the man again.

The list of adjectives was immense and varied. But after that night in the Great Hillston Cemetery, you could add one more word to the list.

Pregnant.

Nine months later, she gave birth to a healthy baby boy. She named him Lancelot.

Lance, for short.

1995

PAMELA BRODY HAD NEVER KNOWN HER PARENTS. SHE'D been put up for adoption at birth and had been unlucky enough to draw the short straw in regard to her new adoptive guardians. An alcoholic "father" and neglectful "mother" had managed to keep her alive for the first four years of her life, but, as the social services worker had put it in Pamela's case file, it was nothing short of a miracle the girl had survived.

Malnourished, dirty, and living in a suburban façade of a home that was nothing but despair on the inside, Pamela had been rescued a month after her fourth birthday after a neighbor had peered over a backyard fence one afternoon and saw the girl walking around naked, unsupervised, and eating a stick of butter.

"She was singing," the neighbor had said when asked if there was anything else he'd like to add. "She was singing that song from *The Wizard of Oz*. The one about the rainbow. But she only kept repeating the first part."

After being saved from the nightmare of a home she'd started in, Pamela had bounced from foster home to foster home, before finally ending up in the Home for Girls. It wasn't that she misbehaved or was disrespectful. All the foster parents simply shrugged their shoulders and confessed it was as if Pamela had no interest in being a child, or letting them be parents. She was withdrawn and acted as if other people weren't there. She sat at the dinner table for meals and said her pleases and thank-yous, but conversation was brief and forced.

Everyone agreed the only time Pamela looked truly happy was when she had a book in her hands.

She lived at the Home for Girls and attended school and made decent grades. The Home for Girls wasn't some run-down *Oliver Twist* disaster full of beatings and rationed food, but instead a dull, quiet place. State employees who cared just enough to keep the job—because it certainly wasn't the pay keeping them from jumping ship—and enough tax money and donations throughout the year to keep the home hospitable and comfortable enough for those few young women who had nowhere else to go.

Pamela made some friends at school but didn't socialize as often as most teachers would have liked. She wasn't odd and wasn't made fun of—no more than your average high schooler, that is—but most agreed she was simply uninterested in most of the things that a regular fifteen- or sixteen-year-old woman might be. She seemed happy enough and was pleasant enough to talk with—quite funny at times, actually—but it was as if her head was always in the clouds. She dated some, but it never amounted to anything serious . Living at the Home for Girls made having boyfriends difficult, if not impossible at times.

At age eighteen, the very next day after her high school graduation, Pamela Brody packed a small bag and walked out of the Home for Girls and never looked back.

The first time she looked into the face of her newborn baby boy, the memories from her early childhood—memories a therapist might be surprised she could remember, given how young she'd been—resurfaced for the first time in years, and she quickly shoved them away and promised herself, promised her son, that she'd be the best mother she could possibly be. She promised she would do anything to keep him safe.

She swore Lance smiled back at her as she had the thought.

And for these first two years, as she watched Lance sit in his high chair and smear the chocolate frosting from his birthday cupcake across his face, occasionally sticking his fingers in his mouth and sucking at the sweetness, Pamela Brody felt she'd been upholding her promise fairly well.

Lance always had clean clothes and a clean diaper. He never went hungry. He had toys—mostly secondhand items from thrift stores or gifts from friends—and had already developed a fascination with books, albeit big bright ones made of cardboard and full of pictures.

Pamela managed to balance her work schedule and coordinated with friends to make sure Lance was cared for at all times. She refused to take him to a daycare—it was too much like a group home in her mind. Sometimes this meant having to drop shifts and have a few less pennies in the paycheck come payday, but they always managed to make do. Money and material possessions had never mattered much to Pamela Brody. Life mattered. Happiness mattered. Her son mattered.

And Lance was a what you'd call a dream child. Even in his early days, he cried very little. He didn't throw tantrums or fits, didn't wail incessantly for hours for no reason. He usually sat quietly in his playpen or his swing or his high chair and simply looked content.

Most people would also agree that Lance's eyes seemed to be the eyes not of a child, but of a person much older, much wiser. If you really looked at the boy long enough, you almost felt that he was looking right back at you, and then deeper. As if he was connecting with you on a level you really couldn't understand or believe.

Pamela Brody had told one of her closer friends—Lizzie, who worked with her at the town's library—that sometimes she was certain she could actually communicate with Lance by looking into his eyes. She said sometimes, when she was feeding him and he refused whatever she was offering, turning his head and pursing his lips or spitting it out once tasted, she'd stop and look at him and simply concentrate on the question "What is it you'd like to eat then?" And if she thought hard enough about it and could keep her concentration, suddenly, like a clown springing out of a jack-in-the-box, the image of carrots, or applesauce, or sweet potatoes would pop into her head as clear as day. And Lance would eat it. Every time. "See?" she'd told Lizzie one day during their lunch break. "He can *tell* me what he wants to eat."

Lizzie, though polite, had nodded and changed the subject.

But though Lance was well behaved and intellectually advanced—as far as Pamela Brody was concerned—she also couldn't deny that there was something else going on with her son, almost as if he had managed to learn a secret he was holding on to, unable (or unwilling) to tell her.

Sometimes, while the two of them played or read together, Lance's attention would snap away from whatever they were involved in, his eyes darting to some unoccupied space in their living room or kitchen and locking on to something intently. Pamela would follow his gaze and see nothing—a chair or a lamp or the stove, everyday items Lance ignored ninety-nine out of a hundred times. He would stare for long moments, Pamela's voice or her actions unable to snap him out of whatever trance he'd fallen into. Sometimes Lance would smile, giggle even, as he looked into nothing. This bothered Pamela for reasons she couldn't quite put her finger on.

But not as much as it bothered her when her son's eyes would suddenly go wide with fear. Those moments sent chills down her spine, causing her to scoop Lance up in her arms and rush him into a different room or leave whatever building they'd been visiting or shopping in.

But the worst moment for Pamela Brody, the moment that solidified her ever-growing suspicion her son was legitimately seeing things that she could not, came in the middle of the night when Lance was eighteen months old.

She was awakened by the sound of Lance crying, loud sobs that made her own throat feel raw. She jumped from bed, threw on her robe and crossed the hallway to Lance's small bedroom. The small nightlight plugged into the wall socket was still there —she could see its faint outline by the light of the moon coming through the slats of the window blinds—but it was not glowing. Just a darkened, empty plastic shell.

Lance's cries tapered off as soon as Pamela entered the room, growing quieter and quickly becoming just soft moaning and whimpers. She rushed across the carpet to his crib, ready to reach down and scoop him up.

Her arms and hands froze mid-scoop.

Lance was standing in his crib, his tiny hands gripping the bars and peering out.

He was facing away from her, his back turned to her and his gaze fixed on the corner of the room where the old wooden rocking chair sat. This was where Pamela would rock him to sleep at night or sometimes sit to read books as he napped, occasionally peering through the bars as he slept and letting her heart fill with joy at the sight of him.

As Pamela's eyes adjusted further to the dim light, she took one more step closer to the corner of the room, ready to reach out for Lance and ask him—though she knew he could not answer, as least not with words—what he was looking at.

She stopped again. Felt ice in her veins.

The rocking chair was just beginning to settle, slowly creaking back and forth, back and forth.

As if somebody had just left, quietly sneaking away.

While the event with the rocking chair had caused an uneasy feeling that would not dissipate until the sun came up, Pamela Brody was much more curious than concerned.

After only a few minutes of rocking Lance in the very chair in question, she laid her son back to sleep in his crib and slipped out of the bedroom. But she did not sleep. She went to the kitchen and made herself a cup of tea and sliced a small sliver of the pie she'd made yesterday. Then she sat at the kitchen table and lifted the mug to her lips and felt the steam rise across her face. She sat like that for a long time, slowly sipping, and thinking about everything that had seemed different about Lance from the day he'd been born.

She knew that people with special cognitive abilities were abundant on earth—those with greater senses of perception or memory or awareness than others. And she would have no problem admitting that Lance might very well be one of those people. But she felt he was also *more* than that. The intense stares that could seemingly communicate thoughts and ideas across brainwaves were a prime example of this. That bordered more on telepathy than simple awareness and perception.

And then, of course, there were the distant stares, when he would fixate on things that simply were not there for such lengths of time. Pamela considered the rocking chair again, the way it had impossibly rocked in the still room. Then she very quickly, right there in her small kitchen with a plate full of pie crumbs and a mug with the cold leftovers of her tea, accepted that Lance wasn't staring at *nothing*. He was simply staring at things the rest of the world couldn't see.

Pamela felt a chill wash over her at this realization, and she quickly turned around in her chair and stared back into the living room through the kitchen entryway, as if she'd suddenly noticed that she wasn't alone in her own home in the middle of the night.

There was nothing in the living room. No shapes or shadows scurrying out of sight. The battered recliner was still upright and unmoving. The afghan was still draped across the rear of the couch where she'd left it.

She carried the empty plate and mug to the sink and washed them both, then headed down the short hallway to her bedroom, carrying with her not a sense of fear, but what she could only describe as some unusual sense of pride.

Pamela Brody did not believe in coincidences. Lance was hers for a reason.

My boy is special, she thought as she laid her head against the pillow, hoping to squeeze out a few hours of sleep before starting her morning routine. *And I need to be ready for him.*

After Pamela Brody's early childhood and uninspired adolescence, Lance, and whatever abilities he surely possessed, felt like a peace offering from the universe.

1999

LANCE CONTINUED TO BE A HEALTHY CHILD, AND AS HIS body grew, so did his abilities.

Pamela often relied on him to find missing items around the house—keys, purse, sunglasses—and while most folks would admit Lance seemed to be able to locate missing household items quickly, often they would not admit it was because he was using some sort of extra sense, a mind-tic that guided him to the correct location. Not that Pamela often inquired about other peoples' opinions of her son. She had made a decision the night of the rocking chair incident, just before she'd fallen to sleep, that whatever made Lance different—*special*—it was probably best to keep the information to herself. If people became scared or worried or maybe a bit too curious, it could mean bad things for Lance. For Pamela. Images from a number of science fiction movies had popped into her head, sad and frightening pictures of children with wires and electrodes and sensors strapped all over their head, locked away in cleanrooms with men in white coats all looking on stone-faced and waiting for results, pens hovering over clipboards.

Her son was a human being. Not an experiment.

Aside from being a mental bloodhound and helping Pamela locate lost items, Lance's telepathic link with his mother also seemed to be getting stronger. Pamela would occasionally test this by thinking of simple questions and concentrating on her son.

Are you finished eating? she would think, sitting across from Lance at the kitchen table, watching him fork the last bits of food into this mouth.

"Yes, ma'am," he would say, acting as though nothing unusual at all had just taken place.

Eventually, Pamela graduated the testing to things a little more strenuous. She would stand in the kitchen while Lance was in his bedroom reading and ask him, *I'm about to make a pie. Do you want to help?*

And sure enough, a few moments later, she'd hear the bedroom door open, followed by Lance's footsteps coming down the hall.

It was exhilarating.

It was terrifying—but in the best of ways.

Pamela Brody was not one to fear the unknown. She embraced all walks of life and all things philosophical and all ideologies. She worshipped life and all its mysteries. How lucky was she that her son was perhaps one of the greatest mysteries of all?

And he only kept surprising her with more gifts...

On one Saturday afternoon three days before Thanksgiving, and roughly a month before Lance would turn five, the doorbell of their small home rang—a tired-sounding chime barely audible over the sound of a teakettle that had just begun to scream. Pamela moved the kettle to a different burner and headed toward the door, wondering who could be visiting. Lance had been in the living room, coloring on the floor, and when she entered the room, he didn't look up to her, but simply said, "Bad man out there, Mama."

Pamela Brody froze on the carpeted floor, watching Lance use a red crayon to color in Spider-Man's suit. Meticulous. Well within the lines.

The doorbell's chime gave it another go, and Pamela stayed put.

Only when she heard a mumble from the other side of the door, and heavy footsteps walking down the wooden porch steps, did she venture toward the door and peek out from a window. A man in a sport coat and blue jeans was just past their mailbox and headed down the street.

The next day, a Hillston sheriff's deputy had stopped by and asked Pamela if she'd seen a man walking around the neighborhood yesterday. Apparently the man was going door-to-door claiming to be accepting cash donations for the local soup kitchen to help provide for the needy on Thanksgiving. He did not, in fact, work for the soup kitchen or any other charitable organization and had managed to disappear with roughly five hundred dollars in stolen cash.

Bad man out there, Mama.

As Lance had grown out of the infancy and then toddler stages of his life, his shifts in focus, those times when his eyes would lock on to things unseen by others, the sporadic flashes of fear and concern across his face, dwindled away. By the time Lance was five, although Pamela Brody had certainly not forgotten those moments from Lance's life and would *never* forget the night of the rocking chair incident, she could now go days, sometimes weeks, without having the thought cross her mind.

All that changed on the first official day of summer in 1999.

School had been out for a couple weeks, but Pamela and Lance had done their lessons earlier that morning—Pamela having decided to homeschool Lance herself, at least until grade school. She wanted to develop a better understanding of her son's abilities and intellect and personality before subjecting him to the harsh reality of the public school system. But mostly, she wanted to protect him as long as she could.

It was a beautiful day, the sun out and the weather warm but not sweltering. An occasional breeze blew in their faces as they walked hand-in-hand down the street, headed toward the park. Lance had a junior-sized basketball under one arm, while Pamela carried a basket with a light lunch, a blanket, and a paperback novel she would try to finish while Lance played.

Though today she wouldn't be able to help herself from keeping an extra eye on her son. Not after what had happened a week ago.

Last week, on the local six o'clock news, the pretty blonde behind the anchor desk had put on her serious face and alerted everyone that three-year-old Alex Kennedy had gone missing. He had last been seen playing in his sandbox in the Kennedys' backyard, which was no more than three-quarters of a mile from the Brodys' house, as the crow flies. Mr. Kennedy had run inside to answer the telephone and returned ten minutes later to find his son nowhere in sight.

Proclamations of child abduction ran rampant. Doors and windows were double-checked at night by parents across the entire town. Peaceful Hillston had been shocked awake.

There had been constant reminders on the news each night. The sheriff's office had held a press conference with Mr. and Mrs. Kennedy onstage, looking pale and exhausted and hardly aware of their surroundings. Mr. Kennedy looked particularly ill. Pamela could not imagine his guilt. If Alex Kennedy was never found, the man's ten-minute mistake would haunt him for the rest of his life.

So far, no leads had surfaced.

But Pamela tried not to let the event deter her good mood. Lance had done very well with his lessons today, and the look of excitement on his face as he carried his basketball toward the park was enough to make her smile big and warm her heart. She hoped to be able to save up enough money by Christmas to be able to buy a cheap hoop for the driveway.

Birds sang overhead.

Today was a good day.

They entered the park and followed the jogging trail north, which would give them a nice walk past the baseball fields, wrap them around the pond, and then deliver them to the basketball courts. There were two covered picnic pavilions near the courts, but Pamela always preferred to spread her blanket out under one of the nearby trees.

There was a softball game being played on the first field, cheering parents absorbed in the action.

Joggers ran by, folks with dogs tugging on leashes, snouts sniffing and tongues hanging.

On the playground, squeals of delight echoed, swing set chains squeaking, and footfalls on the wooden bridges spanning the play area.

They walked, shoes crunching on the trail's crushed gravel. Lance had pulled away from her and walked ahead, tossing his ball in the air as he went, looking back occasionally to make sure Pamela was still close by.

As they rounded a bend and began to pass the pond, Lance stopped.

Pamela stopped too, waited. Sometimes—though rarely—Lance liked to watch the ducks splash in the water. But this interest had waned as he'd gotten older.

Pamela looked toward the water. She saw only a single other person nearby, a man on the opposite side of the pond, fishing pole cast and cooler at his side. The ducks—only three today—were near him, perhaps hoping for some tossed bread.

Lance was looking right, toward the other side of the pond, where there was nothing but grass and a small wooden dock that served hardly any purpose. He began to walk.

"Lance," Pamela called, her voice barely above a whisper.

She could feel it. She couldn't understand or articulate it, but she could sense something off in her son at that moment.

Rocking chair.

She followed Lance as he made his way toward the dock, doing her best to stay close, but also not interfere. She was curious, and a small part of her scolded her for risking her son's safety to satiate her own curiosity. But she knew Lance, knew he was smart enough and well behaved enough not to do something to jeopardize his life.

Though there was now another part of her that was going to make absolutely sure and sign him up for swimming lessons at the local YMCA as soon as she got the chance.

Lance continued toward the dock, then slowed, veering slightly left and walking toward the water's edge.

Then he did something that made Pamela Brody's heart stop.

The water rippled as a strong gust of wind blew across its surface, and Lance raised his hand and waved.

Waved at nobody.

Waved at nothing but the empty pond.

Then he stood still for a full minute, the basketball once again tucked under his arm, his eyes locked on to the water.

And Pamela knew. She knew before he spoke a single word. Maybe it was her direct connection to her son's mind; maybe it was a sudden full realization of what Lance's abilities truly were. But she knew. All the same, she knew.

Lance turned and looked at her, his face pure innocence. "Mama," he said. "That boy from TV is in the water. I think he needs help getting out."

Alex Kennedy's drowned body was pulled from the pond later that day.

Later that evening, a sheriff's deputy who was only a few weeks on the job was sent to the Brodys' house to ask questions.

His name was Marcus Johnston. He'd gone to high school with Pamela, and they talked for hours that night. Marcus left with much more information than he'd expected. Information he would likely take to his grave. Secrets he would keep for a girl he hardly knew.

Because for some reason Marcus Johnston couldn't quite nail down, it only seemed to be what was right. And in a world so full of wrong, a little more right seemed like an okay thing to provide.

2010

"I'm telling you, Lance, it's my bloodsucking ex-wife! Is the alimony not enough? She's got to come steal from the store, too?" Nick Silverthorne's face was the color of a tomato, and he pulled at the thinning hair atop his head. "I mean, I knew she was lowlife ... *trailer trash.* But I can't believe she'd have the goddam balls to come in here and steal from me. Like she didn't get enough in the divorce? Bloody hell, Lance, never get married."

Lance Brody leaned back in the musty chair in his boss's office. Nick Silverthorne had owned the Hillston Sporting Authority for nearly twenty years, with two additional stores in surrounding counties. He'd done well for himself. A smart man who could always swing a deal and always turn a profit. He'd just happened to get caught up with the wrong woman early in life and then have said woman consistently increase his blood pressure while decreasing his bank account.

Lance's mother had said she hadn't been surprised to learn of Nick Silverthorne's affair. "I imagine a man can only take so much of a particular blend of crazy."

This was about as much of an insult as Pamela Brody offered toward anybody. Lance had smirked when she'd said it.

"Sir," Lance said, "with all due respect, why haven't you installed any security cameras in the store yet?"

The Hillston Sporting Authority's security system consisted of deadbolts on the front and back doors, an in-floor safe in the back office where Lance and Nick Silverthorne were currently sitting, and the super complex password of Password456 on the store's computer.

"Do you have any idea how much those damn things cost?" Nick asked. "I put a few in the new stores, you know, since I can't always be there to keep an eye on things, and I about fainted when I got the bill. No, sir. We've never needed those things in Hillston, and we don't need them now."

"Sir," Lance said, "we're getting robbed. So—and again, I say this with all due respect—don't you think we ... well ... sorta do need them now?"

Lance had worked for Nick Silverthorne since his freshman year of high school, and after three years of learning his boss's nuances and tics and mood swings, he felt comfortable enough saying such things. Being on the Hillston High School varsity basketball team as a freshman had made Lance a bit of a local celebrity, and Nick loved bragging that Lance spent a lot of his off-season and after-school hours in the store, helping guests and keeping things running smoothly. Still, Lance felt the air change in the room slightly, and he uncrossed his long legs, bumping his size fifteen shoes on the front of Nick's desk. He stood, stretching his back. At six foot six, he had a hard time with a lot of chairs, could never quite get comfortable.

Nick Silverthorne stared down at his desk and thought about Lance's comment. He shook his head. "She's not even taking that much," he said. "It's like she's just doing it to annoy me."

"Didn't you get her key back? When you all ... you know?"

"Of course I got her key back! Doesn't mean the bitch didn't make more before she returned it."

"And you didn't change the combo on the safe?"

Nick Silverthorne glared at Lance. "Why would I change the combo if I didn't think she could get in the store?"

Lance glanced at the clock on the wall. He had to get going. He was helping set up for the girls' volleyball game. All members of the basketball team had to volunteer to help at other sporting events, and tonight was his night to work. Not that he minded. There were worse sports to watch than girls' volleyball.

Lance shrugged. "You're right, sir. Of course. Have you called the police?"

Nick shook his head. "Not yet. But if she thinks she can just keep getting away with this..." He sighed. "I know, you've got to go." He stood from behind the desk. "See you tomorrow?"

Lance nodded. "Yes, sir. I've got the morning shift."

Nick was about say something but stopped, then said, "Thanks for letting me vent about the ex. I know it's not your problem. Just nice to scream for a bit sometimes, you know?"

Lance thought about the many conversations he'd had with his mother over the years. Conversations he could have *only* with her. "Yes, sir. I do."

Nick nodded. Smiled. "Okay, get out of here." Then he held out his balled fist toward Lance, expecting Lance to bump it. It was a gesture that Nick Silverthorne appeared to be about a decade too old for, but Lance always obliged.

Only this time, when Lance and Nick's knuckles met, Lance was hit with an instant flash of events, some deep-down and locked-away memory from the depths of Nick Silverthorne's mind. Something the man obviously had no ability to bring forth into his current state of consciousness.

Otherwise, he would know everything. Just like Lance did now.

Lance had to suppress a chuckle as he left the office and headed off toward the high school.

Lance had no idea why making contact with some people caused those instant-download moments. And often it was not a one hundred percent occurrence with the same person. Take Nick Silverthorne, for example. Lance had bumped knuckles, shaken hands, punched shoulders, and slapped high fives with Nick a thousand times over the past three years, and never once had he been gifted one of Nick's memories or gotten a vision of some snapshot from Nick's life.

It was unexplainable. Just like all Lance's other gifts and abilities. The confusion and frustration that surrounded Lance's talents sometimes caused him so much anguish he would sit awake for hours at night, asking questions to the darkness and always circling back to the heaviest of questions: *Why me?*

There was no answer. Not from his mother and not from the universe.

Lance supposed he could have asked his father if the man had any inclination as to why Lance was the way he was. But Pamela Brody had never even so much as told Lance his father's name. She'd been honest enough about the situation—blunt, in fact—telling Lance his father was a one-night stand and that the man had literally run away after the deed was done. She always told the story with a laugh, but Lance was always left feeling empty. Not because he didn't love Pamela and appreciate her ability to raise him as a single mother and make sure he had everything he ever needed in life, but because he still had questions. He always had questions.

He was left with nothing but simply accepting who he was. No further explanation needed. It was the only way to cope and survive.

Every night, though, he went to bed longing to be normal.

He'd seen things nobody should never have to see. He knew things that most people were never supposed to know.

Sure, his gifts came in handy, and sometimes even allowed him to have some fun, but there was a dark current running beneath all the light. Always there, always lurking.

The darkness was what scared him.

The following morning when Nick Silverthorne arrived at the Hillston Sporting Authority, he found the front deadbolt unlocked and the music already playing from the overhead speakers. Lance was behind the counter, sitting on a stool and staring down at a laptop Nick had never seen before. He had a bemused look on his face.

"Morning, sir," Lance said, waving.

Nick walked to the counter. "You're here early," he said. "Your shift's not for another hour."

Lance shrugged, grin still on his face. "I wanted to show you something."

Nick searched Lance's face for an explanation. "Okay."

"One of the girls on the volleyball team is in the A/V club. They help record all the school events and produce our truly terrible morning announcement pseudo-news show. She let me borrow this." He pulled a clunky video camera from beneath the counter and set it down. "And this." He pointed to the laptop.

"Okay," Nick Silverthorne said again.

"I'm know I'm only supposed to unlock the store when I'm first one here in the morning, or if there's an emergency," Lance said, "but I thought I would try and help you figure out what's been happening to the cash from the safe." Lance looked sheepish, almost coy, as if there was something he wasn't quite letting on about.

Nick's eyes narrowed to slits. "So you came back here last night and what? Camped out?"

Lance smiled. "Sort of."

"Why the hell do you have that stupid grin on your face?" Nick said.

Lance spun the laptop around so the screen faced his boss. "Press the space bar."

Nick looked at the screen and saw a full-screen video already loaded. He hit the space bar and watched, slackjawed, as the on-screen version of himself strolled through the front door of the Hillston Sporting Authority wearing pajama bottoms, brown slippers, and a ragged Hillston High School t-shirt. He walked across the floor, moving in slow, almost exaggerated movements, shuffling his feet and teetering from side to side, almost as if he were drunk.

The on-screen Nick approached the door to the store's office and the camera followed, keeping a good distance behind. After a minute, the camera got closer and peeked inside the door frame. On-screen Nick was hunched down by the in-floor safe, mumbling over and over to himself as he spun the dial. "*Gotta pay the bitch, gotta pay the bitch, gotta pay the bitch.*"

The Nick Silverthorne of the present widened his eyes as the on-screen Nick lifted the lid to the safe, reached in and retrieved one of the bank bags. He unzipped it and rifled through it, pulling out a handful of twenties and sticking the rest back in the bag before replacing it and the top of the safe. He spun the dial and stood up.

On-screen Nick retreated the way he'd come, exiting through the front door of the store and locking it.

Nick Silverthorne's eyes looked slowly from the screen, met Lance's. "What in the hell?"

Lance couldn't help himself. He laughed at his boss's disbelief. "You're sleepwalking, sir. You're stealing from yourself!"

Nick Silverthorne was quiet for a full minute, glancing from Lance and back down to the screen where the video sat frozen, finished. He blinked a few times, as if clearing his thoughts, and then started to laugh louder than Lance had ever heard the man laugh before.

"Why in the hell didn't you wake me up, you asshole!"

Lance clutched his stomach, laughing so hard it started to hurt. "I ... I think I heard somewhere you're never supposed to wake somebody sleepwalking. It can screw with their head or something."

Nick pointed at the screen. "How much more screwed up can I get?"

The two of them laughed some more, and when the raucous noise finally died off, Nick thanked Lance for solving the mystery before he went and called the police on his batshit crazy ex-wife.

"I coulda sworn it was her," Nick said. Then he scratched his head. "Shit!"

"What?" Lance said.

"I know who the thief is, but I have no idea where I'm putting the money!"

The laughter broke out again.

Later that day, as Lance was finishing his shift, Nick called him back into the office. On top of the desk was a hiking backpack that sold for almost as much money as Lance made in a single paycheck. Nick pointed to it. "New models should be coming in in the next couple weeks. We need to dump the existing inventory, have a markdown sale."

"Sure," Lance said. "How much?"

Nick shrugged. "I'll figure it out. But you take that one."

Lance was genuinely surprised. "Seriously?"

Nick picked up the bag and tossed it to Lance. "Yes. Payment for keeping me from looking like a fool."

Lance caught the bag and examined it, grateful. "Thank you, sir. I mean it."

Nick nodded. "I know you do, son. I know. Now get out of here and go have some fun with the rest of your Saturday."

2015 (I)

A FEW WEEKS INTO THE FALL OF 2015, THE TEMPERATURES had finally subsided from blistering ninety-degree days to a more acceptable seventy-five. When the sun began to set in the evenings, things cooled off even further, dropping to mid- to low sixties, creating that much-loved fall chill. The kind of chill that made you think of pumpkin spice everything and flannel shirts and brightly colored leaves. The kind of chill that made you snuggle up to your loved ones on the Hillston High School bleachers for Friday night's football game and sit inside for your Saturday morning breakfast out at the cafés, instead of on street-side patios or courtyards.

An unmistakable change came when summer ended and fall began. Along with the change in weather came a change in lifestyle. People began preparing for the upcoming holidays— first a choice of Halloween costumes, then what size turkey to buy, and finally whose house would be hosting Christmas dinner and which church service would best fit a family's schedule on Christmas Eve. The pools closed. Men who could usually be found on the golf courses or out fishing on the week-ends were suddenly self-sequestered indoors, huddled around television sets and devouring as much college and pro football and potato chips as their wives would allow. Women were rarely spotted in the wild outdoors without a cardboard-cupped latte or hot chocolate.

All these things happened almost instantly, an unspoken, natural transition. All these things were welcomed, especially after such a brutal summer of heat and dryness.

But in Hillston, Virginia, there was another big event to signify the beginning of fall: Centerfest.

Centerfest was a large celebration held in the downtown streets one day a year. The festivities were always held on the exact date Hillston had been founded. This year, it would be a Wednesday. A nuisance to some, but tradition was tradition.

Both local and out-of-town vendors set up tents and booths to sell every imaginable art or craft. Food trucks smoked and steamed and fried and grilled all variety of mouthwatering items, filling downtown with a mixed aroma of charbroiled sweetness that would cause even the fullest of stomachs to grumble for more. Carnival-like games were set up—the basketball hoops with overinflated balls, the impossible-to-knock-over cans, basket and ring tosses, balloon darts—all the expected entertainment displaying rows of large stuffed animals as prizes, which few people were ever spotted actually carrying away from one of the booths.

There was live music and face painting, and the local fire department put on safety demonstrations. There was a makeshift petting zoo sufficient for only the smallest of children.

Centerfest was Hillston's biggest event of the year, and people always looked forward to it. Not because of the five-dollar sand art their kids could build or the three-dollar funnel cakes, but because the air was always cool and crisp, and the company was always good.

For Lance and Pamela Brody, this year's Centerfest would be the day that would forever change their lives.

2015 (II)
(THE REVEREND AND THE APOSTLE SURFER)

Three days before Centerfest was when Lance saw the Reverend for the first time.

The Hillston Sporting Authority had been very busy for a Sunday afternoon, but Lance hadn't been surprised. The last few days before the official start of the PeeWee and Rec League football and soccer seasons were always a madhouse in the store as procrastinating parents rushed in on their lunch breaks and piled through the door after work to quickly buy all the supplies their son or daughter needed for the first game or first practice. Nick Silverthorne always loved it. "A rushed shopper is a shopper who doesn't care about the price," he always said.

Lance had seen the evidence to support this claim.

But as Lance had left the store at just past six thirty on that Sunday evening, leaving Nick alone to finish out the day and lock up, he'd seen something else. *Someone* else. Someone he'd never seen in Hillston before.

A block east of the Hillston Sporting Authority was a small café that did big business. Lance knew the owner—Mary Jennings—and had graduated with her daughter, Kate. Mary had started Downtown Joe ten years ago with a menu that consisted of coffee and croissants. Now she ran an operation that employed a dozen people, had a full-service breakfast and lunch menu and cozy indoor or outdoor seating. It was *the* only spot most Hillston residents thought about when they wanted to go out to grab a cup of coffee. Being as close as it was to the store, Lance had spent much of his own money at Downtown Joe, and every time he said hi to Mary, he told her to tell Kate hello.

Kate was away at college, just like most of the other kids Lance had grown up with, and probably had a hard time even remembering Lance's face when—if—Mary ever actually delivered his greetings.

Lance wondered what his life might be like right now if he'd left Hillston. What would he be doing right this moment if he'd accepted one of those basketball scholarship offers? Would he be at the gym, working on his game? Would he be at the dining hall with friends—new friends—devouring plate after plate? Or maybe he'd be at the library with the cute girl from his History of Western Civilization class, supposed to be going over notes for the next day's big quiz but both really just flirting and waiting for the other one to suggest they hang out again sometime, somewhere other than a library with open notebooks in front of them.

But he hadn't gone.

Couldn't.

It was too unpredictable. His gifts, his curse, they'd developed over the years, and while he might never fully understand them, at least in Hillston he'd grown to learn what to expect from them. And in Hillston—sleepy, tiny Hillston, Virginia— things had already been bad enough.

Lance had grown up seeing the lingering spirits of the dead —some nice and well dressed and seemingly at peace, despite their continued presence among mortals, but others ... others appeared in a form resembling the moments of their deaths, or worse. Car crash victims with dented faces and necks that hung at unnatural angles, arms and legs twisted and snapped with bones popping through skin. Murder victims with knife wounds gaping open between shredded bits of clothing, or bullet holes—small and black and sometimes so innocuous-looking it was hard to believe it was enough to end a life—peppering their torsos or marking their temples. Cancer patients who'd finally succumbed to that deadly disease, their bodies emaciated and always heartbreaking.

Lance had seen more than just the human spirit. He'd also seen the evil beyond the veil. He'd seen things from a world that was not ours, a place where suffering and pain were the fuel on which entities thrived. Call it Hell, call it Purgatory, call it Walmart on Black Friday—the things that came from this other place were things that no person should ever have to see.

He'd seen all these things—*endured* all these things—and he'd never even gone any further from home than away games with the basketball team and a few short day trips with friends.

Friends that were gone now. Friends that had moved on to real lives that stretched beyond the Hillston county lines and had infinite possibilities.

And then there was his mother....

How could he ever leave her?

It wasn't that she was incapable of taking care of herself—far from it! She was one of the most capable and strong women Lance had ever met in his life. Yet ... there seemed to be some bond between them that was deeper than just your normal mother/son variety. It was as if on some deep-down level, some place that existed far beyond anything our human minds were meant to comprehend, Lance and Pamela Brody coexisted. They survived because of each other.

Or maybe it was because she wasn't just Lance's mother, she

was his best friend. A best friend who knew everything that he was.

A friend who would never leave him.

The Reverend derailed Lance's regretful thoughts of what-could-have-beens.

He sat alone at one of the wrought-iron patio tables outside of Downtown Joe. He was tall and thin and sat ramrod straight in his chair, a black dress shirt tucked neatly into black dress pants. Dress shoes, scuffed and worn, flat on the ground, his knees bumping the underside of the table. Lance could see the white collar insert peeking from beneath the shirt's fabric as he came upon the man from the rear, and as he passed by and turned to look at the man's face, he saw the single white flash on the man's otherwise completely black outfit, right there at his throat.

He's a priest, Lance thought. *Some sort of minister ... or reverend.*

His face was clean-shaven and smooth. Pale, as if he hadn't seen the sun in a year's time. Despite the man's thinness, loose skin drooped around his neckline, and wrinkles dissected his forehead and grew from the corners of his eyes. His nose was large and curved, like a crescent moon. He could be forty, he could seventy. It was hard to tell with the thick crop of gray hair he wore parted on the side.

The Reverend was taking a delicate sip of coffee, steam rising from the cup, visible in the cooling evening air. His other hand was placed flat atop a small leather-bound black book that rested on the table, as if he were about to swear an oath.

Lance kept walking and then turned the corner at the end of the block, taking one last peek at the man before he disappeared from view. The Reverend placed his coffee cup back on the table and reached for the little black book, flipping to a specific page and starting to read.

See you soon, Lance.

The words invaded Lance's mind and disrupted his thoughts like an alarm waking him from a drowsy morning sleep, a sudden burst of awareness that snapped awake the brain in an instant state of confusion. Lance came to a stop on the sidewalk, his sneakers nearly skidding on the concrete. He stood silently and looked all around, checking for anybody, looking for any possibility that the voice he'd just heard had not originated inside his own head.

But he knew it had.

There was no question. Lance knew better than to try and explain the unexplainable. Some things were just better left accepted and unquestioned. His entire life, for example.

Somebody had just sent him a message—*See you soon, Lance*—and there was no mistaking the voice's tone.

It had been a threat.

And then, there on the sidewalk, a slow trickle of dread grew and spread through Lance's body. He breathed in deeply, gathering his resolve, then turned and walked back toward the street he'd turned from. He rounded the corner and stared back down the block toward Downtown Joe. The patio table was empty. Just a white ceramic coffee cup with a couple dollar bills pinned beneath it, loose ends flapping in the breeze.

Lance stood there on the corner of the block for a full minute, watching the faded green bills do their dance in the wind, and then he heard the motor—a slow, whining purr of an engine making its way slowly closer, echoing along the walls of the buildings near the other end of the block.

And then it emerged, slowly revealing itself bit by bit as it appeared from behind Downtown Joe, crossing the street perpendicular to Lance. An antique Volkswagen bus—something Lance had only seen in movies and TV shows. It brought to mind grainy film and faded colors and waves and sand and

41

shirtless guys who said *dude* and *totally* and had long hair and didn't own a pair of shoes. Something from the seventies, maybe sixties.

The bus was two-toned, the majority of its body a Creamsicle orange, with white accents along the windows and top. And sure enough, as if the universe was playing some sort of cosmic joke with Lance's thoughts, in the driver's seat was a man with blond hair down to his shoulders. The skin on his arms, protruding from his sleeveless t-shirt, was the deep reddish-brown color reserved for only a select few groups of people—lifeguards and construction workers among them.

Also surfers and your general variety of beach bum.

The van disappeared after crossing the street, swallowed by the downtown buildings. Its low-whining engine faded away into nothing.

Lance stood still long after the bus was gone.

See you soon, Lance.

The Reverend had been riding shotgun.

———

Dread followed Lance home.

He walked the streets and sidewalks he'd walked hundreds of times in his life, a path home he could practically follow blindfolded, but he wasn't alone this time. This trip home was different. This trip home—in a way Lance could only recognize as the part of his brain tuned into the things unseen, unspoken— seemed to carry some extra weight to it, as if it were somehow important ... or maybe final.

But the dread was there, for sure. Lance felt it there, growing in his chest as his sneakers beat the concrete and asphalt. Felt its coldness spread through him along with the soft breezes rustling the treetops as he approached his neighborhood.

Things had changed.

Changed in a way Lance knew could mean nothing good.

See you soon, Lance.

The voice, the tone, the underlying threat. All three of these things would be worrisome enough, but they weren't what bothered Lance, weren't what had him swiveling his head back and forth with each step, eyes scanning for the Creamsicle Volkswagen bus.

Lance had read many peoples' thoughts throughout his life, caught glimpses of their memories and secrets and current state of mind. Often, it was accidental. Even more often, it was as if the universe, or whatever power controlled the universe, granted him these access key cards into peoples' minds when it was needed the most. Lance didn't know why—just another item on the unexplainable list that was his life—but figured it was that a full-time pass into the minds of others would perhaps be too great a power—too great a temptation—for even the strongest-willed human to handle.

Lance had always been the fisherman in these thought-retrieval episodes. Casting his telepathic reel and seeing what he could hook.

Today was the first time in his life somebody had ever found their way into *his* head—other than his mother. With his mother, he'd always assumed it was the mother/son bond that sometimes allowed them to communicate with each other. And even in those instances, which had become fewer over the years, it still seemed to Lance more like his mother simply sent him an invitation to read her mind, a mental text message that Lance could retrieve and read if he desired.

Today with the Reverend had been different. Today, it felt as if his mind had been invaded, as if the man outside of Downtown Joe had sliced open Lance's brain as easy as a hot knife through butter, had pried open a gap and shouted his message. No resistance, and no waiting for approval. He'd kicked in the door and stomped into Lance's mental house.

And he'd done it from nearly a block away.

All of this brought Lance to two terrifying conclusions.

First, the Reverend was extremely powerful. Lance didn't know how far the man's gifts reached, but his ability to deliver his message into Lance's mind spoke volumes.

Second, the message itself, with its tone and the manner in which it was delivered, along with its implications, meant that the Reverend—and possibly the Surfer—knew what Lance was. Maybe not completely, but enough.

And they were coming for him.

Lance walked up his porch steps and opened the front door. Stepped into the living room.

His mother was in the kitchen, singing softly, her voice meshing with the occasional clang of a pan, or the whipping of a spatula. The smell of apples and cinnamon and sugar wafted throughout the house. The windows were open, and the house was almost chilly, the curtains flowing in the breeze. A row of candles were lit on the mantel above the fireplace, autumn scents like pumpkin and leaves.

God, Lance loved his home.

Loved his mother.

Which is why, when he walked into the kitchen and said hello, finding her folding a crust atop a pie they would likely share together later tonight, along with coffee and tea, and she asked him how his day was, he lied.

"It was fine. Busy day at the store, but nothing unusual."

It was the first time he had ever lied to her.

It would also be the last.

Lance and his mother had each had two slices of pie as they read together in the living room, and Lance had washed his down with two cups of coffee.

But it wasn't the caffeine that was keeping him awake now. It wasn't the fear of the Reverend, either—at least not completely.

It was guilt.

Lance had lied to his mother for her own protection. That was how he was looking at it. That was the only way he could somewhat justify his actions in his mind. Yet his dishonesty sat uneasily on his heart, churned in his stomach. His mother had always been there, a helping hand held out and a voice of reason waiting to speak, throughout all the dilemmas and discoveries and outright bouts of confusion and anger Lance had displayed throughout his life. And he would be eternally grateful to her. At times even felt he was undeserving of her patience and perseverance with him.

So why lie? Why now?

He didn't want to upset her, that was one reason. No child ever wants to send their parents into a panic. Parents are extremely protective beings, ready to fight and claw and scrap and find solutions. Lance simply didn't want his mother to begin to dread and worry about his situation until he perhaps understood it in greater detail. Maybe Lance was overestimating the magnitude of what had happened on the street outside of Downtown Joe. Maybe the Reverend was in Hillston to *help* Lance. Maybe he knew of others with Lance's gifts and was ready to lead Lance to the support group he'd desperately desired his entire life.

Unlikely.

But there was one thing of which Lance was certain—

mostly certain, that is. Whether the Reverend was out for blood or out for peace, his interest was in Lance. Not Lance's mother. If things did get bad, if things did turn toward the darkness that Lance knew all too well roamed the earth, it was better that he be the one it came after, not Pamela. He wouldn't be able to live with himself if something happened to her because of him.

It's not her fight, Lance thought as he finally slipped off to sleep. *It's mine.*

Lance did not sleep well, his slumber disrupted by a nightmare of him running through a dense crowd. A street, downtown Hillston, packed tightly with people who were all smiling and laughing and not even noticing him as he plowed through them. He could smell fried foods and sugar in the night air, could hear a band somewhere close by, speakers blasting electric guitars and the *thump thump* of the drummer's bass. The hair on the back of Lance's neck was prickling, electricity running through his veins. He ran through the masses, no idea where he was going, a strange, terrible emptiness filling his chest as he went.

He woke up sweating, his sheets twisted and his pillow half off the bed. The sun was up, slipping through the blinds, and Lance smelled bacon cooking and coffee brewing.

He smiled. His mother always brewed him coffee, even though she never touched the stuff.

This small token of his mother's love sent a fresh wave of guilt through him as he stood and dressed and went out to the kitchen.

He'd taken three steps into the living room when he froze. He heard it first, the familiar whining purr of an engine. A noise he would never forget in a million years, though he'd only heard it once before. And once the sound reached his ears, his head jerked toward the front windows, which his mother had open, the chilly morning air enough to make him shiver. He caught just the tail end of a vehicle turning at the end of the street, headed back toward town.

A bus.

Creamsicle orange.

"Lance? Everything all right?"

He turned at the sound of his mother's voice. She stood in the entryway to the kitchen, a fluffy white robe wrapped tightly around her, those ridiculous toe socks on her feet. Rainbow-colored. "You look like you've seen something."

Most folks would have said, "You look like you've seen a ghost," but not Pamela Brody. She knew better. With Lance, the answer could very well be "I did."

Lance did his best to smile. "I'm fine," he said, walking toward her. "But I can definitely use some coffee."

Lance did not leave the house all day. Instead he stayed in and tried to read and tried to watch TV and tried to take a nap. But he was only half-committed to any of these tasks. His mind was always on lookout, always checking out the windows, waiting to see Creamsicle orange. Waiting for the Reverend.

See you soon, Lance.

Aside from the Volkswagen sighting early Monday morning, nothing else had happened to set Lance on alert. His day had been a miserable mesh of paranoid hours, his mind racing, searching, trying to dissect and make some sense of what he'd seen, what he'd been told. He'd been incredibly unsuccessful, and after the uneventful day, by Tuesday morning he was ready to go out, determined to try and get some answers, find some clues.

His shift at the store started at nine thirty, but after saying goodbye to his mother, he was walking through the door of Downtown Joe at just past eight fifteen. By then, the before-work coffee grabbers should be gone, and he was hoping to have a chat with Mary Jennings without a lot of eavesdropping ears.

The bell above the door chimed as Lance stepped through, and he held the door open for Mrs. Vargas, who was in her sixties but looked as though she could be forty. A cougar if there ever was one, she was dressed in yoga pants and a hoodie, expensive running shoes on her feet. Cardboard cup of coffee—nonfat, no whip, no sugar, for sure—in one hand.

"Thanks, handsome," she said as she passed by, touching Lance's arm with her free hand. Lance was hit with a sudden image of Mrs. Vargas lying in her bed, naked, with Will Sanders fumbling in front of her, struggling to pull off his pants and join her.

Lance let the door close and laughed under his breath.

Will Sanders was only a year older than Lance and had been the basketball team's second-best player. He was currently attending Virginia Tech. Lance had seen him in town last summer when he was home visiting. He wondered if that was when ol' Will had decided to test the whole "with age comes experience" theory.

Cougar indeed, Lance thought, then wondered if the universe had shown him that image just to put a smile on his face. Boy did he wish he understood how any of this stuff worked. He needed a manual.

Downtown Joe smelled like heaven, if your idea of heaven was full of coffee grounds and pastries. The tabletops were clean, the floor had been freshly mopped, and the display cases full of freshly baked goods were so crystal-clear and smudge-free they were practically invisible. They whole interior had been outfitted for fall: scarecrows and pumpkins and wreaths made of orange and yellow leaves. The chalkboard menu's largest item was the Pumpkin Spice Latte. "Better than Starbucks!" the sign proclaimed. Lance believed it.

Mary Jennings was behind the counter, reaching into one of the display cases with a gloved hand and pulling out a slice of banana bread, placing it in a small bag and handing it to the man at the register. "You know you're making me fat, Mary," the man said, taking the bag and handing over some cash.

Mary smiled. "And you know I take that as a compliment."

The two shared a quick laugh together and the man took his banana bread and left, leaving Lance and Mary alone in the café, the music playing softly from the overhead speakers— country today—and a coffeemaker humming and buzzing as it brewed into a fancy new pot.

Mary saw Lance and smiled. "Morning, Lance. Be right with you, I need to grab a pan out of the oven. Back in a jiffy." She twirled, the apron she wore puffing out around her waist, and then disappeared through a door that led back to the kitchen.

Lance stood, listening to Kenny Chesney strum a guitar and sing about summer love, and heard some clanging noises from the back as Mary did her work. Now that he was here, Lance was uncertain exactly how to proceed. He'd come seeking answers, but what was he going to ask? He wanted to know more about the Reverend. Anything. What his name was, where he was from, when he'd gotten into town, heck, what kind of coffee he'd had. Right now, the Reverend was a complete mystery, a stranger with at least one shared gift with Lance—the ability to get into other people's minds. Though admittedly, the Reverend appeared to be more powerful than Lance in this regard.

Mary might suddenly think him crazy, coming into her store and asking after a customer from two days ago. But certainly she'd remember the man, right? He wasn't a resident, that was a fact—small-town benefit, you know almost everybody—and his look had been quite distinctive. As Mary reemerged from the back, Lance tossed his self-consciousness aside. He knew he had to get whatever information he could out of her, even if she thought him rude or prying or strange.

"In a little early today, Lance. How's Pamela?"

Lance smiled and stepped closer to the counter. "She's great, thanks for asking."

"Wonderful. I keep meaning to swing by the library and see what books she's got to recommend for me—she's so *good* at figuring out what I like to read—but it's hard to get away from this place. You know?"

"Sure," Lance said. "People love it here. You should be very proud."

Mary's face reddened. "Thank you for saying that, Lance. You're always such a sweet young man. Now what can I get you today? The usual?"

"Yes, please. That would be great."

Mary nodded and grabbed the fancy coffeepot, filling the largest cup Downtown Joe offered. She popped a lid on it and slid it across the counter to Lance. "On the house today, sweetie."

Lance started to protest, but she cut him off. "Don't even try, mister. You're one of my best customers. Loyalty should be rewarded, right?"

This sounded very much like something Lance's mother would say. He stopped his attempts to pay and simply said, "Thank you. I appreciate it."

When he didn't turn to leave, Mary eyed him with a curious look. "Is there something else, Lance?"

Lance stood, feeling the warmth from the coffee cup in his

hand and trying to find the right words to ask his questions. Mary's look went from curious to concerned, and just before Lance could speak, the speakers overhead let off a sudden burst of static—a quick second of digital fuzz—before the music came back into focus.

Only it was no longer country. Kenny Chesney had been silenced.

Now the song playing was "Surfin' U.S.A." by the Beach Boys.

Mary's brow crinkled, and she looked up to the speakers in the ceiling. "Well, that's odd."

The realization of what the song was sent ice washing through Lance's veins just as the bell above the door to Downtown Joe chimed and Lance heard footsteps fall in line behind him. And not normal footsteps you'd expect to hear in the fall weather—not sneakers or boots, but the sticky slap of rubber against skin. Flip-flops.

Mary Jennings's face lit up with a smile. "Well, hello again! I didn't think you'd still be in town."

"Can't say I did either, babe," a voice that sounded as if its owner had just finished smoking the world's largest joint said from behind Lance. "But it seems we've got a bit of gnarly situation on our hands. The boss man is pretty sure we'll get it taken care of soon, though, so no worries, right? We'll be catching a wave out of here in no time."

Lance turned around and stood face-to-face with the Surfer. The man who'd been driving the Creamsicle bus. He looked at Lance with eyes that were as blue as a pristine ocean. "How's it goin', bro?"

Lance took a step back. He was a good six inches taller than the Surfer but felt entirely too close, suddenly revolted by the man's presence. A feeling as though the man were literally covered in some sort of slime, a sickly substance that radiated off him and affected anybody too close. There was something wrong with the Surfer. Something bad.

The man wore bright blue board shorts and a sleeveless yellow t-shirt, his hair now pulled back into a small ponytail. The flip-flops on his feet were grimy with dirt. He stared at Lance with a sort of dumb grin, waiting.

"I'm well," Lance said.

The Surfer nodded. "Righteous." Then he turned and asked for an iced latte.

Lance thanked Mary again for the coffee and left Downtown Joe. He made his way to work, locking the door behind him and keeping it that way until the very second the store was supposed to open.

Lance spent the following hours distracted. Customers came and went, each chime from the bell above the door caused Lance's head to dart that direction, poised and ready to see the Reverend or the Surfer coming to fulfill their promise.

See you soon, Lance.

But each new arrival to the store proved to be no threat, just another regular Hillston visitor looking for new hiking boots or a new softball bat or a jockstrap. Lance mindlessly performed his duties, easily managing to smile and act like himself as the customers carried out their transactions. All the while, his thoughts were focused on what had happened with the Surfer this morning in Downtown Joe.

The music, for starters. There was no way that was a coincidence, the odds of the station that had been playing glitching like that, only to land on a channel that just happened to be playing an oldie about surfing just as the Surfer had walked through the door. No way.

His mother's words echoed in his head. "The universe is too smart, too calculated for us to accept the concept of a coincidence, Lance. Do you, a person with your gifts, honestly believe things could be so random?"

No, he couldn't. His mother might have some quirky ideals and thoughts, but this one was a bit Lance tended to agree with.

And who *was* the Surfer, really? The darkness and pain and evil that had seemed to radiate off the man had been enough to cause Lance to stagger back, doing all he could not to run in revulsion. The Surfer was somebody bad. Someone who had done terrible things. And that trick with the music? He certainly had some sort of special ability. If there had been any doubt in Lance's mind that the Reverend wasn't here to pay him a friendly social visit, the Surfer had completely erased those doubts.

But why don't they just come? Why are they slowly revealing themselves to me?

And that's when two scenarios occurred to Lance. One, the Reverend and his Apostle Surfer were testing him, trying to see if Lance was really who they believed him to be. They were giving him clues, dropping breadcrumbs to lead him to their intentions, and when Lance confronted them, they'd be waiting.

Or two ... and this scenario slammed into Lance's gut with such a force his head felt dizzy and light with fear ... they were misleading him. Distracting him.

Maybe the message didn't imply they would arrive for him. Maybe he would come to them. And the only way Lance could think of that he would willingly go somewhere the Reverend and Surfer were waiting for him would be....

His mother.

Lance quickly recalled his mother's work schedule. She didn't work today and wasn't scheduled to volunteer at the YMCA either. She'd be at home. Alone. And because of Lance's dishonesty, she was completely unprepared for anything or anyone bad to show up. Completely unaware there was a new evil in town, and it was coming after the Brodys.

They'd played him. They'd set him up and gotten him so worried about himself, he'd forgotten all about the people around him.

Lance bolted from behind the counter, calling out, "Is anybody still here?" When nobody answered, he rushed to the door, flipping the hanging sign from OPEN to CLOSED and rushing out onto the sidewalk, barely remembering to lock the door behind him.

He ran with everything he had, crossing streets without looking and ignoring the few blaring horns from the sparse morning traffic. His legs were still strong, but his lungs burned, his stamina not what it used to be during his playing days. His heart was pounding in his ears as he turned down the street into his neighborhood and kicked into another gear he wasn't sure he still had. His head swiveled all around, eyes peeled for the Creamsicle orange.

He was close now, one more block. He could see his front yard, and at the sight of it, he had a very strange, yet very normal thought. *I'll need to cut the grass one more time this year.* And then he almost laughed at having such a trivial thought during what could be such a pivotal moment in his life.

He ran through the grass and bounded up the porch steps, slowing just enough not to knock the front door off its hinges. He threw open the door and stopped.

His mother sat on their living room sofa, a mug of tea in one hand—Lance could smell the lavender and honey—and an open book on her lap. She saw his face and instantly asked, "Lance, what is it? What's wrong?"

Lance scanned the room, saw no one but his mother. Felt a soothing relief.

"Lance?" she asked again. "Tell me."

So he did.

They'd gone into the kitchen and Pamela had sliced Lance a piece of pie, pie he hadn't thought he wanted yet somehow had managed to eat half of before he'd even begun to tell his mother what he'd been keeping from her. There was still coffee in the stainless-steel pot, and she poured him a cup and reheated it in the microwave, setting it beside the pie plate. He took a sip without thinking. It was too hot and had gone bitter, but he drank it all the same.

Finally, Pamela sat down at the table across from him, a fresh mug of tea cupped in her hands. "When you came home two days ago, I could tell something was wrong. You know me, Lance. I've never pushed you to tell me things you didn't feel the need to, and I won't change now. You're the smartest boy I know, and I trust your judgment."

Guilt.

The heaviest of guilt plowing through his gut.

He began with an apology—which his mother quickly and almost sternly dismissed—and then filled her in on the Reverend and the Surfer. All that had happened.

"Funny song to pick as entrance music, isn't it? The Beach Boys? How old is this man?"

"That's the part that bothers you?" Lance asked. "I picked up one of the worst vibes ever from this guy and you're concerned about his taste in music?"

"It's just peculiar, that's all."

Lance finished his pie. "That's the whole story," he said. "I don't know when, and I don't know why, but I know they're going to come for me. They know what I am, and they want me."

"For what, do you suppose?"

"Does it matter? Clearly nothing good. Otherwise, wouldn't they have, I don't know, just introduced themselves to me instead of quasi-stalking me around town and sending me telepathic messages with severe threatening undertones?"

Pamela nodded. "Fair point."

Lance waited for her to say more. He was not rewarded. Finally, he asked, "So what should we do?"

His mother looked at him and smiled. "Nothing."

"*Nothing?*"

Pamela stood from the table and placed her empty mug in the sink, then turned to face him, leaning against the counter. "Lance, what do *you* suggest we do? Run? Flee our home, our lives?"

"Mom, I *know* they're dangerous. Trust me."

She nodded. "Maybe so, Lance. But that doesn't change my question. Yes, they're dangerous. Well, guess what, some might call you dangerous, too, given your gifts." She held up a hand before he could protest. "Yes, I know, not a fair comparison. What I'm trying to tell you is you seem so sure this is a battle you're going to lose. Why is that?"

"I ... I don't know."

"A feeling? Your instinct?"

Lance closed his eyes and searched for that feeling he'd carried with him as he'd run home from work. Remembered the disgust he'd felt at the aura of evil that had oozed from the Surfer. Remembered the way the Reverend's message had slammed into his head with zero resistance.

"It won't end well," he said finally. "I can't explain it—"

"You never can."

She smiled at him, but he couldn't bring himself to return the favor. "I can't explain it, but this is different, Mom."

"How so? We've been through some whoppers over the years, Lance."

"That's the worst part. I honestly can't tell. It's like the picture is fuzzy, and all the pieces are scrambled. I just can't help feeling—and this is the part that scares me the most—like this is the end of something."

Pamela Brody had a heck of poker face. She only stared and nodded, her face unflinching at her son's news.

"But also," Lance said, "it might be just the beginning."

They were quiet for a long time then, both trying to wrap their minds around everything they'd discussed. Finally, Pamela walked over and placed her hand on Lance's shoulder, leaned down and kissed the top of his head. "Maybe it's both, Lance. Maybe it's both. Either way, this is all part of it."

"Part of what?"

She smiled at him. "Whatever it is you are. This is the way it's supposed to be."

"Even if they kill me?" He was starting to become irritated with her apparent ignorance to the true danger of the situation. Her reliance on fate or destiny or whatever master plan she believed his life was following.

"You're not the only one with an instinct, Lance," she said, walking back into the living room. "You've got something they don't fully understand yet."

Lance and his mother spent the rest of Tuesday evening inside. Pamela made a chicken pot pie for dinner—one of Lance and his mother's favorite diner-type foods—served with fresh rolls, and Lance couldn't tell if she was simply trying to appear as though everything was normal between the two of them, of if she honestly, deep down, had no concern in regard to what Lance had revealed to her earlier over the tea and coffee and pie.

As he helped her clean up after dinner, he came within half a breath of telling her he thought they should leave. Not forever, but just for a few days. He had some cash saved up—not much, but enough—and they could go on a mini-vacation. Someplace a few hours away, where they could find things to do to take their minds off the Reverend and the Surfer, and maybe avoid whatever altercation was sure to be headed Lance's way. He'd call the bus station and see what was available for the next day.

But would that work, really? They'd found him once, couldn't they find him again? Could the Reverend track Lance with his mind, the way Lance sometimes found himself tracking down lost items, or walking in a certain direction without really meaning to, only to find himself exactly where he needed to be? If Lance had that kind of power, it was quite possible the Reverend had it at exponentially greater levels.

Lance just didn't know. So he'd stayed quiet. Finished with the dishes and then excusing himself to his bedroom. Feeling sick and lost.

His mother called out after him, "Are you excited for Centerfest tomorrow?"

They went together every year. Lance, of course, once he'd gotten to be about eleven or twelve, would always arrive with his mother but then drift off to walk around with his friends, trying to show off at the games to win pretty girls prizes, but he'd always find his way back to her. It was essentially a tradition.

"Sure," Lance said. "I could sure go for a funnel cake right now."

He closed his bedroom door.

Lance awakened just after seven on Wednesday morning, and the moment he opened his eyes, he felt it. The feeling, the instinct, the verification. It was going to happen today.

They would come for him. He was certain.

The Hillston Sporting Authority was always closed on the day Centerfest was held. "No point," Nick Silverthorne always said. "Half the people who come in off the street just want to use the bathroom, and the other half just want to get out of the sun for a bit. Nobody comes to buy anything. Might as well keep the doors locked and enjoy the day. I do love a good fried Twinkie."

Lance hadn't disagreed.

He dressed and found his mother in the kitchen, much like he did most mornings, and when she turned to look at him, he felt another wave of grief, an unexpected sadness.

Pamela handed him a mug of coffee. "Today?"

Lance nodded.

"But you don't know what?"

Lance shook his head.

Pamela smiled. "Well, we won't let that ruin the day, now will we?"

And that's when Lance felt something different: a fresh, warm blanket of happiness and love. He looked at his mother and marveled at her resilience and optimism. Her faith in him—his abilities—was absolute. Her belief that he was walking a predetermined path was unwavering. Whatever happened today was supposed to happen, and it would not be Lance's last challenge. That was the way she saw it, and nothing was going to change her mind.

Lance sat at the table. *I'll fight. I'll give everything I have because I can't let this woman down.*

The hours ticked by slowly, and Lance spent most of them in his room, trying to shake the oddest of feelings, an annoying drip at the base of his brain that was telling him to take a good look around, because he'd never see this place again.

He'd prove the drip wrong. He'd prove it all wrong.

But when his mother told him she wanted to leave in a half hour's time, Lance couldn't help but feel like a death-row inmate who'd just been told he'd be taking his last walk very soon. No matter how hard he told himself otherwise.

I'll be back here tonight, he told himself. *Whatever happens, it'll be okay.*

But it never hurt to be prepared.

Before he left his bedroom and met his mother at the front door, he did two things.

One, he called Marcus Johnston—now the mayor—whose number he'd had memorized since he was ten years old, and told him to expect a call tonight, because Lance might need help. The mayor pressed for more, but Lance gave him nothing else. Because honestly, what he could he say?

And two, he grabbed his backpack from the floor by his closet, tossed in a few items, and slung it over his shoulder.

Then he met his mother in the living room, and they both headed out the door for the last time.

They walked together down their street, already able to hear the low murmur of noises coming from town. A cacophony of far-off voices. An indeterminable genre of music being played through powerful speakers.

The air was cool as the sun began to set behind the horizon. Breezy. Lance felt goose pimples along his arms and watched his mother pull the sleeves of her sweater down over her hands. She didn't question his backpack. Didn't say a word until they got closer to the actual event. They continued on, silently, and as Lance looked around at his surroundings, seeing houses and landmarks and trees he'd observed his entire life, the silence between him and his mother seemed to say it all. "This has been our life together," it said. "And it's been wonderful."

But tonight, it might very well come to an end.

These heavy thoughts weighed Lance down as they walked. The burden he'd carried with him since he'd been born suddenly seemed to take on more heft than ever. Lance didn't subscribe to any particular organized religion, but he'd read the Bible. As they walked and Lance contemplated the events which might be about to come, he thought about the story of Jesus in the garden of Gethsemane the night of his capture. What must it have been like, knowing, waiting? Ripe with the knowledge that only you could perform what needed to be done, whatever that may be.

After Jesus, he thought of Aslan, the great lion in Narnia, who'd so willingly and confidently strolled through the White Witch's mocking crowd, head held high as he arrived to sacrifice himself.

Am I that brave? Lance asked himself. *Am I at all worthy of these gifts?*

The voices and the music got suddenly louder and Lance came back from his thoughts and found that they were standing at the end of Church Street. The block or two of Church that was dedicated to Centerfest was full of people. They milled about from craft tent to craft tent, from booth to booth. Ahead, Lance could just make out a glimpse of Main Street, running perpendicular to Church. Main Street was the main artery of Hillston, and thus Centerfest. Plumes of smoke and steam rose over the roofs of the buildings, and his stomach, despite the situation, grumbled with hunger.

There was no way his mother could have heard his stomach,

but as if on cue, she reached out and touched his arm, saying, "Before anything else, let's get you that funnel cake."

She smiled at him, and Lance was again hit with an overwhelming urge to convince her to leave with him for a while, to leave whatever was about to happen in Hillston for somebody else to deal with.

But of course, there was nobody else. And Pamela was already making her way through the crowd, headed for Main Street. Lance followed her, his head well above most of the other patrons out this evening, following the top of his mother's head as she made her way forward. The air continued to grow cooler, almost rapidly, as the sun finally disappeared completely and the streetlights and shop lights became all that lit downtown Hillston. His mother spilled out onto Main Street, and Lance turned left to follow her toward the rows and rows of food vendors. Brightly painted food trucks with compressors and propane tanks hissing and growling on their rears, torso-sized menu boards plastered on the street side, advertising anything and everything you could ever hope for from a carnival environment. Lance watched a group of small children run by, all holding half-eaten and dripping snow cones, their mouths stained every color of the rainbow. He heard fryers frying and smelled grills grilling. He saw a man wearing a clown suit spinning cotton candy onto a paper stick for an elderly couple standing hand-in-hand, anxiously awaiting their treat with grins on their faces. Lance passed by people he knew, waved and nodded hello. A few looked as though they wanted to stop and talk, but Lance would not stop following his mother. He hated the possibility of appearing rude, but he wasn't letting her out of his sight tonight. Not for anything.

Finally, Pamela stopped in front of one of the food trucks and got in line. Lance came up beside her, looking at the menu board. Aside from funnel cakes, this truck offered fried Oreos, fried Twinkies, fried pickles, fried ice cream, and, seemingly out of place, bottles of water.

"What are you going to have?" Lance asked.

His mother had been studying the board as well. "How do you fry ice cream? That seems inconceivable, don't you think?"

"Cleary some sort of witchcraft, I suspect. Maybe we should go to another truck. I don't want to turn into a toad or have my head shrink after eating whatever they give me."

His mother made a show of thinking about what he'd said. "There'd be less laundry if you were a toad."

Lance grinned. "And less, well, you know, me."

She nodded. "There is that. I do enjoy having you around."

Lance was about to make a witty retort, but found he couldn't. There was a sudden lump in his throat that needed swallowing.

"I'll just have a pinch or two of yours, if that's all right," Pamela said as they stepped up to order.

"Or course."

Lance paid for the funnel cake and they walked further down Main Street, eating their sweet and heading toward the First Bank & Trust parking lot. From the parking lot came a swirling glow of neon lighting mixed with the popping of air rifles and balloons, the clinking of plastic rings against glass bottles and the all-too-familiar echo of basketballs being bounced. The parking lot was home to the game booths.

"I'm finished," Pamela said, brushing powdered sugar from her hands. "The rest is yours."

Lance picked up what remained of the funnel cake, folded it in half, and demolished it in two bites.

His mother watched him. "I'd say I'm impressed—or disgusted—but by now I'm just used to it."

Lance laughed and tossed the empty paper plate into a nearby trash can. "Come on, let's go see if I can get one of these overinflated basketballs into one of these too-small hoops. I love seeing the disappointed faces of the workers when I win."

"Lancelot Brody, that's awful. I thought I raised you better than to revel in somebody else's misfortune."

"Mom, they're ripping people off. You're not meant to win. It's basically rigged."

Pamela considered this. "Really?"

Lance nodded.

"Okay, then, go win yourself a cheap stuffed Spongehead."

"It's SpongeBob."

She waved him off. "Just go win."

Lance did win. He paid two dollars to the man behind the counter at the basketball shoot and then bounced the ball a few times on the ground, getting a feel for it. He tossed it in the air twice, feeling its weight. As expected, it was way overinflated and probably would have landed on the bank's roof if Lance had bounced it hard enough off the ground. Instead, Lance took two steps backward, positioning himself further away from the goal than most of the other participants, and then shot and swished two shots in a row. He didn't even take off his backpack. He did indeed win a stuffed SpongeBob, which he quickly gave to a young boy who had been watching. The boy's parents thanked Lance, and the game attendant gave Lance a sly smile that seemed to say "Congratulations, but now get out of here."

Lance wished basketball was his only special talent. A normal talent that could take him places and that people understood. He'd never forget the confused voices that had come from the other end of phone calls with college coaches when Lance called to politely decline the scholarships they'd offered him. "So where *did* you decide to go?" they always asked. Lance wasn't sure many of them believed him when he said he wasn't planning on going to college. "I'm staying home," he'd say. And then they'd usually hang up.

Lance and his mother stopped to watch a few of the other games but did not play. Lance knew what his mother was patiently waiting for, one of the biggest reasons she came out to Centerfest every year. The music.

Pamela Brody loved live music. She loved the energy from the bands, loved the pounding of the speakers, loved the crowds. She loved how people transformed in front of live music, how their problems and inhibitions seemed to melt when the right song came on and the tune and the beat and the melody carried them to a different place they usually kept locked away, deep down.

She loved to dance.

She'd stand by herself, or she'd join a crowd of other free spirits, and she'd sway and twirl and step along with the music. Her eyes would close sometimes, like a Southern Baptist churchgoer during their favorite hymn, and as Lance would watch her in her long skirts or woven sweaters, with her hair done in braids or sometimes just loose and falling halfway down her back, he would flash to the images he'd seen of Woodstock and smile. She would have fit right in.

He loved seeing her as happy as she was in those moments. Mostly because it made him forget about himself for a while. Lance wasn't stupid. His gifts were a curse not only upon himself, but also his mother. She'd had to deal with things just as much as Lance had. Lance always longed for a normal life, and he couldn't help but wonder—and feel guilty—about whether his mother desperately wished she'd been given a normal child. She'd never indicated such a thing, but then, Pamela Brody wasn't the type of person who would.

He shook himself out of these thoughts and said, "Come on, let's go find the band."

Pamela watched a young girl of about three try to toss her red plastic rings atop the scattering of glass bottles at the ring toss tent, then followed Lance as he led the way out of the bank's parking lot.

They didn't have to search very hard to find the band, because the bandstand was set up in exactly the same place it'd been set up every year since Lance could remember—with the exception of that one time when Lance was about fifteen and some poor sap had mistakenly scheduled the Hillston Farmers Market parking lot to be repaved and lined a day before Center-fest. But tonight, as usual, Lance and his mother walked another two blocks down Main Street and then turned onto Bedford Avenue to be greeted by what seemed like a thousand people packed under the pavilion-like shelters that stretched north for roughly a quarter mile, perpendicular to the street. The city had set up folding chairs under the wooden structures for people to sit and enjoy the show, and while the majority of the seats looked to be filled, there was a massive mosh pit scene spilling out into the parking lot on the other side of the pavilions.

This was where people ended up who just wanted a quick taste of the music before moving on, or those who were young enough and full of enough energy to stand and enjoy the tunes. This was also where people danced. This was where Lance and his mother were headed, he knew.

At the far end of the Farmers Market parking lot, the stage was raised high, a good three or four feet above the heads of the patrons. Speakers as black as night and as loud as jet engines stood like sentinels on either side of the platform, pushing unhealthy volumes of sound out into the night air, permeating downtown Hillston. The band onstage was a local favorite, a young rock group whose sound resembled eighties megastars more than anything more modern, which was ironic since the lead guitarist and singer had graduated a year ahead of Lance. This kid—because he was, after all, a kid in Lance's mind—who now stood onstage singing a Phil Collins cover, to the crowd's delight, was the same kid who'd electrified Hillston High School basketball crowds with electric covers of the day's most popular hip-hop offerings during pregame warmups. He was talented. Lance suspected his band would be playing in venues a lot larger than the Hillston Farmers Market very soon.

His mother took the lead and headed out onto the black asphalt of the parking lot, weaving between clusters of people who stood by, swaying along with the tune or nodding their heads to the beat. She found a small gap in the crowd, a hole that had appeared almost out of nowhere, as if it'd been waiting just for her. Lance followed, trailing just a few feet, and when Pamela stopped in the clearing, which was a little to the left of dead center of the crowd, Lance stopped behind her. She pulled up the sleeves of her sweater now, the crowd and all the walking causing her to grow warmer, and after a few seconds—that was all it really took—Lance could practically see his mother morph into that other person she became in front of the music.

Lance, who was six-six and as graceful as a gazelle on the basketball court, had all the rhythm of a garbage truck. Opting to join the head nodders, he stood back and smiled as he watched his mother get carried away into her special place. During the second song, Martin Hensinger—the local dentist and an avid reader who frequented the library—found his way to Pamela, and the two of them exchanged some small talk and laughed and half-performed a brief awkward dance together before Martin bade her farewell.

Lance had never seen his mother go on a single date his entire life, and again the guilt of her burden pummeled him. How different—how much better—would her life have been?

"Get away from me, creep! Get *away*!"

A young woman's voice struck a chord in Lance's mind, rattled in his head the way the bass from the speakers onstage were rattling his stomach. His vision blurred for a moment, as if he'd been struck. When it cleared, it was as if the music and noises from the crowd had diminished, as if some great hand had turned down the master volume knob on the whole event.

"Help!"

The voice again, coming from his left. Lance turned his head and looked into the sea of people surrounding him. Most were facing the stage, taking in the music. A few leaned toward each other in half-screaming attempts at conversation. They clutched plastic cups of soda or cardboard cups of coffee and hot chocolate (Courtesy of Downtown Joe!). They bit into candy apples and funnel cakes and steak-and-cheese sand-wiches. They all looked happy and relaxed. Nobody seemed distressed.

"Somebody help me! *Please!*"

Lance started in the direction of the voice, stretching up on his toes, occasionally jumping up as he pushed through the crowd, scanning the horizon over the flood of heads.

And then he saw her. Just a fleeting glimpse of a thin teenaged girl dressed in jeans and a Hillston High School hoodie, blond hair splayed out behind her as she struggled. Somebody was pulling her into the alley that ran between the rows of buildings on Main Street and Woodson Avenue. She swung her free arm in an off-balance attempt to attack her assailant, then struggled to turn and get in one last view of the crowd that was seemingly ignoring her cries for help. She opened her mouth, as if to expel one last scream, one last plea, but before she could make a sound, she was violently jerked into the blackness of the alley's mouth.

Lance was moving again now, looking all around him, stunned that nobody had heard this girl cry out. Nobody else was heading toward where she'd been taken. They weren't even looking that direction.

They can't hear her, he thought. *The music is too loud!*

He ran.

But how come I can?

The answer was obvious.

Because of his gifts.

Because of his burden.

Lance Brody was meant to hear the screams because that was his life. He was a light in the darkness. An unassuming protector. Forever obligated, indebted to the world.

Because what was the alternative? Stand by idly and let the world burn? Let the evil win without batting an eye?

What honest human being could do such a thing?

He ran toward the alley between Main and Woodson, not even slowing as he reached the dark slit between the buildings. He bounded in, heart pounding and ready to fight one, maybe two pieces of scum who thought it was funny to violate a help-less young girl. His eyes adjusted to the low light, his footfalls echoing off the encasing walls, and when he saw the scene in front of him clearly, he skidded to a stop so hard the rubber on his sneakers literally squealed against the asphalt, and he had one devastating thought: *I've lost. Just like that.*

Standing fifteen feet away in the shadows of the alley was not a young girl fighting for her dignity and safety, nor was it one or two pieces of scum looking to have some fun by roughing up some innocent bystander.

Standing fifteen feet away in the shadows of the alley, looking as comfortable as ever in his board shorts and sleeveless t-shirt and flip-flops, was the Surfer.

Confusion washed over Lance. He was smart enough to understand that he'd been tricked, baited into a trap like a rabbit in the woods, but he didn't understand how. Who was the girl? *Where* was the girl?

The Surfer smiled at Lance in the darkness, as if reading his thoughts, and that was when Lance was hit with an even deeper realization of the powers he was up against. The Surfer, some-how, had been the girl, or ... had created her ... or ...

What is *he?*

Lance didn't have time to contemplate the mysterious man before him, because just as his mind finally allowed in the instinctive thought to turn and run away, get the heck out of the alley before something terrible, something *final* could happen, he heard the steady rumble of tires over asphalt echoing into the space behind him. He turned halfway, keeping one eye trained on the Surfer, and saw the Creamsicle Volkswagen bus slide into view, completely blocking the mouth of the alley, completely blocking Lance's way out.

The Reverend was in the driver's seat, his white collar seeming to twinkle in the alley's darkness as he stared out the window toward Lance. Past the Reverend, through the van and out the passenger window's glass, Lance could see a blurred and congested image of the crowd in the parking lot, their focus still locked onto the stage, the music. His mother was among them, and Lance wondered if she'd noticed that he'd gone. How long had he been gone? Time had seemed to slow now that he was here, trapped between two foes, but in reality, he'd probably only been gone from the crowd for a minute, maybe less.

Hi, Lance. Ready to go?

The Reverend's voice slid into Lance's thoughts, as smooth as sliding into silk sheets. No hesitation, no resistance.

Just hop on in and we'll go for a ride.

Lance stared back, turning fully toward the bus, his gaze focused solely on the Reverend's eyes. He concentrated and shot back a message of his own, curious to see if it'd be received.

Who are you? Lance asked. *What do you want?*

Lance heard movement behind him and spun around quickly, the Surfer having taken what looked like two steps closer. His hands were at his sides, and he didn't seem to be carrying any sort of weapon, but when Lance remembered the whole damsel-in-distress trick the man had somehow conjured, he wasn't sure any physical weapon would be necessary.

Just make it easy, Lance. The Reverend whispered in his head. *We don't want to hurt you. You're too valuable to us.*

Lance ignored the voice, let his eyes fall over his surroundings, searching for some sort of escape. He clearly couldn't exit the way he'd come in, because of the bus, but he might be able to get past the Surfer and exit out the other side toward Church Street. But still, the thing with the girl, the overwhelming sense of slime and evil he'd felt coming off the man in Downtown Joe ... he was more dangerous than he looked on the surface. Lance didn't want to get close to him—*feared* getting close to him. It was potential suicide.

He saw the handful of metal doors set flush into the wall, service and delivery entrances for the stores and shops, a place for employees to take the trash to the Dumpsters. Each door had a single keyhole and no knob. A small button to ring the bell next to each. They could only be opened from the inside, for security.

Get in the bus, Lance. We have great plans for you.

The music from the stage continued to play, the speakers pumping and the bass thundering. Lance felt his heart pound-pound-pound louder and faster in his head, thought about his mother, out there alone, wondering what had happened to her son, searching for him in the crowd, crying out his name.

Another noise behind him, the Surfer gaining another step.

You're brave, Lance, the Reverend said, and then louder: *But you're ours now.*

Lance's mind spun wildly, desperate for a solution.

And don't worry, we'll take care of your mother.

And just like when a lit fuse finally reaches its end, Lance's temper ignited in a spark of rage and fury that tinted his vision red. His hands balled into fists and his muscles tightened and he poised himself to run straight at the Reverend and jump clear over the Volkswagen if need be. He sucked in one deep breath of air, heard the Surfer begin to move rapidly behind him and....

One of the metal service doors swung open on rusty hinges with a screech that echoed loudly through the darkness. A short man, stocky and balding, stepped out into the alley, freezing when he saw Lance and the Surfer standing outside the door.

"Oh!" he said. "Wasn't expecting anyone out here." The man looked as though he sensed he'd walked into some sort of trouble and started to retreat back inside the building, the metal door swinging slowly closed behind him. Lance sprang into action, the quickness that had been so beneficial on the basket-ball court now helping to save his life. His arm darted out and caught the door and flung it open, hard and wide, the metal slamming into the Surfer's body as he reacted a second too slowly to Lance's movements. There was a dull *thud* as the metal met flesh and bone, and Lance jumped over the door's threshold and quickly spun around, grabbing the door's push bar and quickly jerking the door closed.

"Hey! You can't be in here!" the balding man protested fear-fully. "We're closed!"

Lance didn't even look at the guy, just turned and ran for the front of the store, for an exit. The building was dark, all the lights off save a few emergency overheads that glowed dimly in the gloomy space. These buildings were all old, smelled of must and failed businesses. Lance scanned his surroundings and saw large pieces of wooden furniture in various states of assembly—sawhorses and cans of stain and electric sanders. He pushed through a gray swinging door, emerging into the storefront. He saw an elegantly staged dining room set on his left, a king-sized four-poster bed on his right, wooden tables and chairs and barstools and rolltop desks scattered everywhere. He knew where he was—Hillston Furniture Co.

Hillston Furniture Co. closed at five o'clock every day. Closed on Sundays. Five o'clock had long since passed, and with Centerfest happening, the store had likely been empty for hours. There was absolutely no reason the stocky balding man should have been here, no reason that alley door should have opened.

His mother's words: "Do you, a person with your gifts, honestly believe things could be so random?"

He certainly could not. Especially not tonight.

He thanked the universe for the assist and ran to the front door. The deadbolt was locked, but a quick turn of the thumb latch and Lance was in the street, bounding out into the chaos of Centerfest once again. The noise and the smells and the unknowing people. Unknowing that right now something major was happening, something that could forever change Lance's life—*and who knows what else?*—was going down right under their noses. They were just too busy with their games and food and arts and crafts to notice.

And maybe that was okay.

Lance turned left and ran down the sidewalk behind the food trucks, rounding the corner of Main and Bedford. He saw two things at once: his mother emerging from the Farmers Market pavilions, her eyes locked onto his with a clear under-standing spread across them—*It's happening, isn't it?*—and the Creamsicle bus with its reverse lights on, attempting to do a three-point turn to head toward a small exit ramp, the place where every other Saturday morning, the local vendors and farmers would drive their pickups off Woodson Avenue and back them up to the pavilions to unload and set up shop. It was the only way out with the bus. The rest of the roads were closed off, packed with people and tents. Lance watched it for just a moment, long enough to see the Surfer back in the driver's seat and the Reverend riding shotgun.

Disappointing, Lance. Shouldn't have run. Now it's worse. You'll see.

The Reverend's voice creeped into Lance's head again, and Lance cast out a mental middle finger, raised high. He hoped the Reverend could see it. He hoped it jammed him in the eye.

Pamela was not running, but she walked quickly across the street and joined Lance on the sidewalk. She didn't speak, only looked to him. Lance took her by the arm and hurried up the block, back to the intersection with Main Street. They spilled into the street, people parting around them like a stream around a pile of rocks.

"I saw the bus," Pamela said, her eyes still trying to lock onto Lance's.

Lance was using his height and scanning the crowd, searching for any sign of the Surfer or the Reverend. Though now—a terrifying thought—he wasn't sure he'd actually be able to spot the Surfer outright. The trick with the girl in the alley had changed Lance's entire perspective of what he was up against. "I'm glad you didn't go running toward it like some crazed mother bear protecting her cub."

Pamela gave a slight nod. Somebody bumped into her as they made their way past, and a bit of apple cider spilled from a large plastic cup, just missing their shoes. The person apologized over their shoulder and moved on.

"Something told me not to," Pamela said. "I knew you wouldn't be there if I went."

"Something? Or someone?" Lance asked, finally meeting his mother's eyes.

Pamela only shrugged.

Lance Brody wasn't one to question premonitions or unexplained hunches. Instead, he used his lifetime in Hillston to pull up a mental map of downtown and the surrounding streets, calculated the roads that were still passable and not shut down for the night's events, trying to list all the possible routes the Creamsicle bus could be headed.

They're not done, Lance knew. *They're going to keep coming.*

He mapped out a route back to their house, using a few offshoots down some side streets and one gravel path that ran parallel behind their neighborhood. If he could get back there quick enough, his mother would have some time to grab a few things, and then they could head to the bus station.

Do they think I'll leave town? he wondered. And then, with some disappointment in himself, *Do they think I'm that much of a coward, not to stay and fight?*

But this wasn't running. This was surviving. For both Lance and his mother.

"Let's go," Lance said, pulling his backpack off one shoulder and digging for his cell phone. He flipped open the pay-as-you-go flip phone his mother had given him years ago and dialed Marcus Johnston's personal cell number by memory. He put the phone to his ear and once again took his mother's arm and led her back down Main Street, back the way they'd come what suddenly felt like ages ago. Back toward home. For what might be the last time in a good long while.

Pamela came along after him, but Lance could sense her resistance. He had halfway turned to look back at her, when on the third ring, there was a "Hello?" in his ear.

"It's happening," Lance said. "There's people after me and my mom, bad people. I need you to tell the police to stop an orange-and-white Volkswagen bus if they see one. Just stop the bus and don't let the driver or passenger out of their sight. No questions, okay? I just need enough time to get us out of here."

"Out of here?" the mayor asked.

"Yes."

"Lance?"

"Yes."

"Where are you going?"

There was a tugging on Lance's arm, gentle at first and then more prominent. "Lance," his mother said.

"Home first," Lance said. "Then, I'm not sure where we're—"

"*Lance!*" His mother's voice echoed loudly, causing Lance to stop talking. He glanced around, but none of the other patrons seemed to have noticed or cared. Too much going on. He turned and looked to his mother. She tugged his arm and nodded toward the street stretching out to their left—Avenel Avenue. There were only a few tents set up on Avenel, a couple of jewelry vendors and a man selling pencil sketches of local landmarks. After the first half a block, the street was empty except for the lines of cars parked along the curb on either side, stretching far back into the darkening street. A few streetlights glowed from the distance, and the occasional headlights flipped on as cars pulled out of spaces, headed home. A good stream of people walked in either direction, both toward and away from Main Street—the newcomers, and those who'd had their fill. But the scene was nothing like the packed madhouse of Main Street.

Avenel was where Pamela was pulling him. Lance resisted, planting his weight. "Where are you going?"

"Trust me," she said.

Lance thought out more routes in his head and didn't see how going down Avenel helped them at all, except to get them out of this sea of people. Which Lance actually sort of liked at the moment, as it helped them blend in.

But then he thought back to what Pamela had said to him after he'd escaped from the alley—"Something told me not to. I knew you wouldn't be there if I went"—and crossed his fingers that whatever had intervened with his mother's intentions was taking the wheel now as well. And besides, Hillston wasn't that big. They could get back to the house from anywhere.

And at the end of the day, yes, he did trust her. More than anybody on earth. More than himself.

"Lance?" It was Marcus Johnston in his ear. "Lance, where are you going?"

Lance took one last reassuring glance at his mother and said, "East on Avenel."

"Toward the cemetery?"

Lance felt his heart do something funny, a cold trickle of fear pouring over his head as he realized that if they continued half a mile up the road on Avenel, past the downtown businesses and the few abandoned buildings, yes, they would eventually run into the intersection with White Birch Lane, which led directly to the main entrance of the Great Hillston Cemetery.

"Yes," he said. "I guess so. Just tell them to stop the bus if they see it, okay?" Then Lance ended the call and ran with his mother up the street, toward where—unbeknownst to Lance, and Pamela, too, really—he had been made what he was.

This time, they did run. Both of them together, Lance leading the way with his fingers intertwined with his mother's, trying to keep himself from going so fast that he would end up dragging her. The eyes of the people walking along Avenel stared at them, mouths slightly ajar, curious as to what they were witnessing. Folks looked around, heads darting left and right and up and down the street, thinking maybe something bad was happening—a crazy person with a gun or a knife, or maybe somebody had yelled bomb!—but they saw nothing. Only Lance and his mother running away from Hillston's biggest and best event of the year.

"Maybe she's sick," Lance heard a man say to his wife as they ran by. "Maybe she's going to spew her fried pickles."

Lance had no concern with what people thought. He knew —somehow, he knew—that whatever he and his mother were suddenly caught up in had repercussions larger than any of the folks gawking could possibly imagine.

Lance only wished he knew what those repercussions where. Wished, now more than ever in his life, that he knew what his purpose was, or if he even had one.

The cars continued to line the street three blocks down Avenel, and the people continued to meander and stare as Lance and his mother ran. At the intersection with Vine Street, there were two sheriff's deputies in bright orange vests, one of them holding one of those plastic orange cones used to direct traffic. They were leaning against one of their police cruisers and chatting and watching the people and did no more than glance in Lance's direction when he ran by with his mother in tow. For the briefest of moments, Lance slowed, thinking this was why his mother had wanted to come this way, because she knew there'd be help here. They'd be able to jump in the rear of the police cruiser and have two of Hillston's finest escort them to safety.

But two things happened all at once that caused Lance to forget all that and run even faster, pleading with his mother to keep up.

First, just like when he'd been younger and his mother had mentally asked him to help her find the house keys or sent him the message that dinner was ready while she was in the kitchen and he was playing in his room, Lance sensed her mind knocking on his consciousness's door. He answered and she said: *Don't stop. Not here. They can't help us.*

Second, as Lance slowed to possibly request the assistance of the two sheriff's deputies, he saw a vehicle spit out of the darkness further down Vine Street, tires squealing as it took the right turn too quickly, and its headlights were suddenly pointed directly at Lance, barreling toward him at much higher speeds than the posted twenty-five-mile-per-hour limit.

The deputies turned in unison, jumping at the noise.

The vehicle had appeared quickly, and though the headlights were now blinding, obscuring any clear view of it, Lance had seen enough as it had made the turn.

The Creamsicle bus.

Coming for him.

Fast.

They ran, letting go of each other's hands and sprinting up the street. The deputies were shouting something at the oncoming bus, an incoherent mixture of commands and warnings. People had stopped walking now, half of them staring at the deputies, heads cocked sideways in curious inquisitiveness, half of them watching Lance and Pamela run.

Another block up Avenel, the cars were still lining the streets, but the lot on the right side of the sidewalk was vacant, just an expanse of grass and weeds where Lance had heard McGuire's Pool Hall had once stood in the midseventies before closing and eventually being torn down by the city. Lance pulled his mother in this direction, their feet leaving the hard asphalt and falling softly onto the grass and dirt. They cut the corner of Avenel and White Birch Lane, making a diagonal across the empty lot. To his left, Lance saw more parked cars along the sidewalk of White Birch, which would eventually end as the city street stopped and a rural road began. Ahead and slightly to his right, Lance could make out the looming wrought-iron fence surrounding the Great Hillston Cemetery, a sliver of moon hanging in the night sky above like a winking eye.

Lance risked a glance behind him and saw the tiny silhouettes of the two deputies jump out of the way as the pair of headlights rounded the corner with another squelch of tires and made their way up Avenel.

They've seen us, Lance thought. *We've got to hide. We'll never outrun them.*

They were reaching the edge of the vacant lot now, Lance impressed with how well his mother had kept up, her lean body and long legs striding across the grass with an elegance he'd had no idea she possessed. *Guess I know where I get my athleticism from.* At the far corner, at the edge of White Birch Lane and Route 411, which led toward the county line, was a crushed gravel parking lot tucked away by the side of the entrance to the cemetery. A place for visitors to park and funeral processions to gather on the days of burial. Tonight, it was an overflow lot for Centerfest, and the lot was nearly full, cars parked two rows deep along the edges.

And then he heard the screaming.

He stopped and looked back, watching in horror as the Creamsicle bus sped up Avenel, people jumping and diving out of the way as the headlights tore up the street. The bus was swerving, dodging in half-hearted attempts to avoid pedestrians, but clearly not overly concerned if there was collateral damage.

All because of me, Lance thought. *This is all my fault.*

The bus was three-quarters of the way up the street, making its way toward White Birch Lane. Pedestrians fled in every direction, some jumping on top of cars, some diving back into their cars, others filing into the vacant lot in which Lance and his mother stood. High-pitched shrieks filled the night air, men shouted curses that echoed off the old buildings. The two deputies ran far behind, their arms out, pistols raised in the direction of the bus. But of course they would not shoot. No way. Not with all the people around.

And then Lance was hit with the brilliant idea to turn around and run back the way they'd come and then cut down

Avenel and across Main and head back toward home. They'd be going against the grain, so to speak, but the Creamsicle bus would have to do the same. And with the roads closed off, the Surfer and the Reverend would essentially have to make an entire loop around the outskirts of downtown to get back toward Lance's home.

It would buy him and his mother enough time to get to the bus station, maybe. But, sadly, Lance realized they wouldn't be able to stop at home first. It would be too risky.

He turned to grab his mother's hand and lead her back toward Avenel, but his jaw dropped when he saw that she'd already run further across the lot, headed for the crushed gravel parking lot and the cemetery. She turned and called over her shoulder, "Come on!" Lance said a bad word under his breath but was left with no choice but to follow her.

Lance's backpack bumped and jostled against his back. He reached for the straps and pulled them down in one swift jerk, tightening the bag against him. His mother was only a few feet ahead of him, but Lance felt she was much further. She had an agenda, some deeper understanding of the events unfolding around them than Lance had. She veered right just before they reached the crushed gravel parking lot, and Lance heard the strumming of an acoustic guitar and a male voice singing pleasantly. He looked over the parked cars and saw a man standing in the middle of the parking lot, guitar case flipped open at his feet, standing and smiling and singing to a good-sized crowd who'd gathered around him to watch and listen before heading toward downtown and the main activities. The sounds of the chaos taking place a few blocks away had not yet reached them, drowned out by the man's music and singing, blocked by their turned backs. A young boy maybe five years old ran up to the man and tossed some loose change into the opened guitar case and then ran back giggling to his mother's side.

Lance turned and saw his own mother running along the line of parked cars, headed toward the wrought-iron fence encircling the cemetery, stretching on into the darkness further than Lance could even see. He looked back toward the man playing the guitar and was shocked to see the singer looking directly at him. Still singing, the man winked at Lance, then turned back to his crowd. Startled and confused, Lance turned and ran after his mother. Found her to be impossibly far ahead of him. How long had he stopped and listened? It felt like only seconds, but now his mother had reached the fence and was....

What is she doing? Is she ... trying to climb it?

But no, that wasn't quite right. She was at the fence, facing it, and her hands were gripping the iron rods, poised as if ready to begin to hoist herself up and over. But she stood motionless, her head bowed down, almost as if in silent prayer.

Lance ran to her, his feet suddenly very heavy, his legs feeling as if he were trying to sprint through wet cement. He trudged along, fighting his fatigue. Only a few short yards to go before he'd reach his mother.

And then he stopped, gasped.

The rest of the world seemed to fade away. The music from the parking lot and the sounds from the street and, further away still, the occasional thump of the bass coming from the speakers from the Farmers Market bandstand all vanished. The air grew still and Lance's ears felt as if they needed to pop. It was if he'd stepped inside a giant bubble, one that was shielding out everything except him and his mother ... and the spirits lining the interior of the Great Hillston Cemetery's wrought-iron fence.

There might have been a hundred of them, maybe more. The spirits of so many of Hillston's past residents huddled packed together in a semicircle that stretched deep into the cemetery, deeper than the light allowed Lance to see. But he saw them, lost souls dressed in suits and dresses and outfits spanning decades, centuries. Men and women, young and old, children, and even two dogs who sat quietly at one man's side, as if waiting patiently for their dinner. Every single one of these ghosts had their gaze fixed on Lance's mother.

And every single one of their mouths moved rapidly, as if muttering some repeated incantation or chant, over and over and over.

Lance took a small, tentative step closer, watching his mother as she kept her head bowed, her hands tightly gripping the fence. The mouths of the spirits continued to mumble, mutter, and as Lance stepped closer, he heard indecipherable bits and pieces of their words. It was as if his head were a weak antenna, struggling to tune in to a far-off station that would not come in clearly. He stepped closer still, the spirits' gazes never looking his direction, only locked on his mother. Lance tried to concentrate, tried to home in on the staticky signal of the dead, but found he couldn't. It was as if ... as if he were being blocked, and he understood with a fresh wave of fear that frightened him to his core that he wasn't meant to hear what was being said. The spirits' message was a secret, meant only for his mother.

The squeal of tires on asphalt suddenly burst through the bubble that Lance had seemingly stepped into, and he turned around quickly, his eyes landing on the Creamsicle bus that jumped the curb at the corner of Avenel and White Birch before bounding back over the sidewalk, narrowly missing the front bumper of a parked pickup truck and turning sharply right, headed up White Birch. Heading for the crushed gravel lot.

We've got to get out of here!

Lance turned, ready to rip his mother free from the fence, even prepared to be violent about it if he needed to, but he only froze. Stopped and stood still at what he saw.

His mother stood directly in front of him, a few feet away

from the fence. Tears streamed down her face, falling harder and faster than Lance had ever seen. His mother did not cry, not that Lance could ever remember. He looked quickly over her shoulder and saw that the inside of the fence was empty, just the trees and headstones casting shadows in the soft moonlight. He looked back to his mother, opened his mouth to speak and found he couldn't.

"My boy," his mother said, her voice quivering against her tears, but also filled with … was it happiness? "My sweet boy. Oh, what great things you'll do."

Lance stood, perplexed. "Mom, what—?"

"I am so proud of you. Always remember that," she said. Then: "Tonight is not the end." Then she smiled, reached up and kissed him on the cheek, her tears warm against Lance's skin. Their eyes met then as she pulled away, and Lance saw some final decision being made behind his mother's gaze. "I love you," she said.

And then she ran.

She bolted like a horse out of the gate, taking off away from Lance, leaving him standing alone in the grass by the fence. She ran hard and fast toward the crushed gravel lot and then kept going, back down White Birch. Lance looked on in stupefied awe and shock and disarming fear as he saw the Creamsicle bus plow forward, sprinting, eating up the short distance to the parking lot at a rapid speed, forty, maybe fifty miles an hour. And Lance knew what would happen next. The bus would reach the lot and jump the curb and spill out onto the grass, silhouetting Lance against the fence behind him. He'd stopped for too long, been too caught up in the moment. There was no way he'd outrun them now. They'd run him down in the grass, or they'd trap him against the fence, or … whatever happened, he knew he was caught.

Then he looked back to his mother and was dismayed to see

her suddenly jerk to her right, darting out between the row of parked cars along the sidewalk and stepping out into the street.

"No!" Lance yelled with a voice he could barely find. A strangled cry that didn't even travel far enough for the people in the parking lot to hear.

Pamela Brody had timed it just right. She'd run down the street, keeping herself hidden behind the rows of cars, listening for the noise of the engine, watching the flash flash flash of the headlights filling the spaces between the cars. And then she'd made her move, jumping out in front of the Creamsicle bus as it barreled its way forward.

The Surfer hadn't even had time to hit the brakes. There was no squeal of tires—not until after. There was no blare from the horn, no sudden jerk of the steering wheel in a desperate attempt to avoid an accident.

The front end of the bus smashed into Pamela Brody's body with a noise that Lance would never forget, a crunching of metal and a smashing of glass and the sickening thud of a human body being thrown twenty feet through the air and landing in a crumpled heap on the asphalt.

Now the bus did stop, the tires screeching and the smell of burning rubber filling the air.

People all around, people who'd been diving out of the way and standing wide-eyed on the sidewalk and fleeing for their own safety, began to react. Lots of them screamed, male and female shouts echoing all around. Some fled, desperate not to get involved in whatever tragedy had happened. But others, most, reacted in a way that would later make Lance smile, would help him to remember the good in people at a time when he thought he would never see the good in anything again. They started to run *toward* the Creamsicle bus, which had come to a stop a few feet from Pamela's body, one headlight busted out, the engine purring softly as the vehicle sat motionless.

And that's when the realization of everything came crashing into Lance and he was jump-started again, spurred from his crippling disbelief at everything he'd just witnessed.

"Mom!" His voice was hot now and full with panic ... sadness. "Mom!"

He ran with everything he had toward his mother's body. Already people gathered around her, many of them on cell phones, all placing frantic 911 calls. An angry mob had formed around the bus, knocking on the windows and pulling angrily on the door handles, tugging and jerking and trying to get to whoever was inside and was responsible. The Reverend and the Surfer were now targets. Villains to the residents of Hillston.

And when Lance was within twenty yards of the scene, he saw the reverse lights switch on from the rear of the bus and watched with primal rage as the bus backed up, slowly at first, as a warning to all who might be standing in the way, and then with a quick burst of acceleration that sent people jumping and diving and scattering away. Lance watched in horror as one man had his foot run over. Another's shoulder was hit so hard by the bus's sideview mirror that he spun around like a top before collapsing to the ground in a cry of pain.

The two sheriff's deputies were both on their radios, shouting at whoever was listening on the other side of the connection, and as the bus began to execute another three-point turn and speed off down Route 411, they pulled up their pistols and fired off three or four shots in quick succession, aiming for tires.

They missed.

The bus drove off in a blur of speed, vanishing into the night.

And then Lance was at his mother's side, pushing people out of the way and collapsing on the street next to her.

"Mom," he said, emotions so strong and heavy in his heart he could literally find nothing else to say. "Mom..."

She was flat on her back, one arm bent awkwardly at the elbow. One of her legs twisted grotesquely out sideways. There was blood pouring from her forehead, dripping down her closed eyelids. It ran from her nostrils and spilled from her lips. She looked horrific.

But to Lance, she was still the most beautiful woman on earth. "Mom," he said again.

Pamela Brody's eyes flitted open, bloodshot and unfocused. But she saw him ... deep down, Lance knew she saw him. She coughed, blood bubbling in her throat, and offered a small smile. "Just enough time, Lance. You have just enough now."

There was shouting behind him and then a strong hand fell on Lance's shoulder, gripping it tightly. Lance jerked his head back, turned to find Mayor Marcus Johnston standing there, a look of sheer dismay spread across his face. The sheriff's deputies were on the group now, yelling at people to step back, to get away from the scene of the accident so paramedics could arrive and take over. There were protests, shouts, but Lance heard none of this. His turned back to his mother, found her eyes opened only to slits. She tried to speak, but the noise was barely a whisper. Lance leaned closer, cupping the back of her head with his hand and leaning so close he could still smell the scent of her shampoo and the sweet sugar from the funnel cake over the metallic stench of the blood.

And something his mother had said the day before, a mystery he could not let go unresolved, seemed all at once crucial. "Mom," he said, doing his best to stay strong. "What is it I have? What is it you said I have that they don't fully understand?"

Pamela Brody, despite her pain, despite her life fading from her, smiled. "You have me."

She coughed again, and Lance felt as if his heart had split in two.

"Go, Lance. It's only what's right," she said. Then, with one last breath, "I love you."

And she was gone.

An hour later, after the sheriff's deputies and the paramedics had controlled the crowd, and Marcus Johnston had helped Lance slip away unquestioned—after first tearing the young man away from his mother's lifeless body—Lance was sitting on the seat of a rattling charter bus, his backpack on the seat beside him, leaving his hometown behind.

Pamela Brody had sacrificed herself for Lance for reasons he did not—and perhaps would not—ever fully understand. But there were two things of which he was certain.

One, his mother had learned something from the spirits of the Great Hillston Cemetery. Something that had moved her enough to feel as though she needed to end her own life in order to prolong Lance's. "My sweet boy. Oh, what great things you'll do."

And two, the Reverend and the Surfer were not finished. Lance might have won this battle, but he was acutely aware that this was a war that had just gotten started.

Lancelot Brody, exhausted, drained, confused, devastated, empty, leaned his head back onto the headrest and found himself with no answer to anything other than to try and succumb to sleep. Succumb to the blackness, where hopefully nothing would chase him, and maybe, if he was lucky, he'd see his mother's smiling face again.

Thanks so much for reading DARK BEGINNINGS. I hope you enjoyed it. If you *did* enjoy it and have a few minutes to spare, I would greatly appreciate it if you could leave a review on Amazon saying so. Reviews help authors more than you can imagine, and help readers like you find more great books to read. Win-win!

DARK BEGINNINGS is a 100-page prequel novella and the true beginning of the Lance Brody series – whose first novel is DARK GAME and is available now.

-Michael Robertson Jr

Please enjoy the first chapter of DARK GAME (Lance Brody Book 1) - Available now!

His mother had always told him that a fresh slice of pie and a hot cup of tea was all any good soul needed to temporarily forget their problems. The type of pie and the flavor of tea were of no consequence. Fresh and hot, that was all that mattered.

For the first twenty-two years of his life, Lance Brody had shared many an evening in his family home's kitchen, crowded around the small table with his mother, eating her fresh pies and discussing the way of things. He'd never acquired the taste for tea, however, and preferred coffee for their long discussions. Black. His mother hated coffee, but his substitute of another hot beverage in place of the tea—instead of something from a bottle —seemed to satisfy her.

Alcohol was strictly forbidden in the house. If there was a familial reason for this, Pamela Brody had never told Lance. Nor was religion to blame; the only time Lance's mother ever prayed was when the Bulls were in a tight one with whichever NBA opponent they were competing against, and those prayers were directed at unseen basketball gods who inevitably cared little of an individual's libations. She had no affiliation to the team, nor the city of Chicago. When Lance had finally asked her why she chose the Bulls as her team, she'd simply replied that she liked their mascot. He was funny. Her love of basketball in general was a mystery to Lance, as she'd never played the sport herself, but it was the only organized activity she'd ever encouraged him to participate in throughout his entire upbringing. But the alcohol ... She said it poisoned the mind and the body, and Lance could see no argument against that. He'd never tasted a drop of the stuff.

Not even on the night she'd died where no pie big enough and no coffee black enough seemed adequate to alleviate the pain.

He hadn't cried, not then, and not for most of his life. Crying was something his mother was strangely against. Strange because of how much she stressed being at peace with oneself and understanding and trusting your feelings. She didn't say this the way a condescending therapist might to an uncooperative husband, but in a way that suggested self-strength and confidence. It was what *you* felt inside, who *you* were that mattered in life. "Embrace yourself, Lance. Only then can you fully embrace others." He might have been eight when she'd first offered up this token of wisdom. A typical conversation to have with a second-grader. Typical was something his mother never came close to achieving. She was extraordinary. Not in the same ways Lance was extraordinary—wouldn't *that* have been helpful—but in a way that allowed him the trust and confidence in her to share his world with her and have her love him and help him and stand by his side as he grew and developed in every way you can imagine, and in ways you couldn't.

But now she was dead and Lance was completely alone, stepping off a bus two-hundred and thirty-seven miles away from home with the previous night's horrific events still burning fresh in his tired mind.

He had no plan. Hadn't had time for a plan. The bus was the first one headed out of his town and he didn't care much where it was going. He'd had to leave, been forced to run.

Now he was here.

He was hungry.

Food was as good of a start to a plan as he could think of.

He didn't need to wait for the bus driver to haul his luggage from one of the holding bins along the bottom of the bus. Everything he'd been able to take with him from home was stuffed into his backpack—an expensive thing gifted to him by the owner of a local sporting goods store years ago, when Lance had helped him with a problem—and the backpack had remained in the seat next to him for the bus's entire course. He adjusted the straps over his shoulders, turned and thanked the bus driver for getting them all to their destination safely—an act that was met with a confused expression and mumbled reply that might have been "You're welcome"—and then headed across the street, through a large and mostly empty parking lot, and stopped briefly on the sidewalk.

He breathed in deeply and closed his eyes. Exhaled and opened them. Turned right and started walking, the soles of his basketball sneakers making gentle scraping sounds against the concrete. A warm breeze blew into his face and a warmer sun was just rising above the horizon at his back. He was walking with the traffic, the occasional vehicle slowly passing by on his left. The drivers all looked bored. Looked like they'd rather be anywhere else. It was Thursday morning, so Lance imagined that might surely be the case if they were all headed to a nine-to-five so they could pay the mortgage. *Well, that's* one *thing I don't have to worry about.*

He kept walking.

A mile later, after passing a small strip-mall and a McDonald's, he found what he'd been looking for. The momentary flit of happiness the sight caused him was so brief it might not have happened at all, just a teasing scent carried off by the wind before it could even be enjoyed.

Lance felt something pushing it away.

The diner was called Annabelle's Apron and looked like it

might have been built before Nixon resigned. A rough shoebox of a place with a shiny aluminum front and lots of windows. The roofline looked to be sagging a bit, and there was no telling whether the bright neon signage atop it actually still had any juice left, but there were a few faces on the other side of the glass windows, and all of them were forking food or sipping coffee. Lance stepped off the curb, allowed a pickup truck to back out of a parking space, and then crossed the lot and pulled open the door.

The interior of Annabelle's Apron looked, sounded, and—most importantly—smelled exactly as Lance had hoped. Directly ahead was the long counter with a matching row of stools. A few folks seated there, elbows resting atop the counter as they read the morning paper while they ate. The windows were lined from end to end with booths, the upholstery a bright blue—robin egg, that's what his mother would have called it—and the table tops showed their age, full of cracks and streaks and blemishes. The battle scars of thousands of meals, tens of thousands of cups of coffee and tea and glasses of orange juice and soda pop. The air hummed and chimed with the noise of the kitchen crew working hard, glimpsed sporadically through the open window behind the counter. Two waitresses went to and fro from table to kitchen to table. Smiles plastered on and only a faint sheen of sweat on their brow so far. Hushed conversation and soft playing country music from a lone overhead speaker was occasionally punctuated by the yelling of a young child in the rear-most booth. A location surely chosen as a strategy by its not-our-first-rodeo parents.

And all of this was accompanied by the smells of bacon and eggs and butter and coffee and biscuits.

Lance had been standing at the door for too long, and the woman behind the counter called out as she refilled a patron's coffee, "Sit anywhere you'd like, sweetie. Be right witcha."

He looked over his shoulder, back to the parking lot and the everything beyond it. Scanned the horizon. The sun was higher now, almost full-form. Then his stomach grumbled and he took a seat at the counter, setting his backpack at his feet and taking the laminated menu from the woman who'd told him to sit. The menu was smudged with grease and dried grape jelly, but the text was readable. Lance ordered four scrambled eggs, bacon, hash browns, and a large stack of pancakes. The woman behind the counter—early-sixties, Lance guessed, and with a look of no-nonsense experience creased into her aged brow—looked him up and down one time before asking, "And to drink, sweetie?"

"Coffee, please," Lance said.

She nodded and tore the order ticket from the pad in her hand and turned to post it on the wheel in the window. She spun the ticket into the kitchen where it was quickly snatched by a fleeting glimpse of a cook's hand, and then she returned with a black plastic coffee mug and poured from a full pot. "Just brewed this one, sweetie. You're its first." She winked and asked if he needed cream or sugar.

"No, thank you." Lance said, and did his best to smile.

"Margie, I'll take some of that," a gentleman—a regular, apparently—called from the end of the counter. The woman—now Margie—put a hand on her hip and said, "You've been tryin' to get some of this for twenty-three years, Hank Peterson. Today's not gonna be no different!" This got a chuckle out of Hank and the two other waitresses and Margie went off to fill Hank's coffee.

Lance sat in silence, looking down at the counter and listening to the sounds around him and sipping his coffee as he waited for his food. His mother had always said that diners were some of the greatest places on earth because everything was real —the food and the people. Honest American's cooking good ole American comfort food. The potential of diners always excited her, like each one was an individual mystery just waiting to be unraveled.

Margie refilled Lance's coffee.

His food arrived shortly after.

The bars on the stool were a little too high for him to comfortably rest his long legs—at six foot six, this was the type of problem he'd grown accustomed too—and he had to adjust himself repeatedly to keep his legs from falling asleep. But the coffee was strong and the food was delicious and the general ambiance of the diner did its best to revive his spirits.

Margie cleared his plates when he'd finished. "I wasn't sure you'd be able to eat it all, t'be honest. Large stack usually fills up most folks."

Lance wasn't most folks.

"I don't suppose you'll be wantin' nothin' else?"

Lance was about to say no, but then paused. Said, "Do you serve pie?"

Margie laughed. "You kiddin'?"

"No, ma'am." Lance shrugged and smiled. "I have a high metabolism, I guess."

"We don't set it out till lunch, but I can get you a slice from the back. Apple okay?"

"Is it fresh?" Lance asked, and felt a twinge in his heart.

Margie smiled. "I bake 'em fresh every morning." Then she disappeared into the kitchen and came back a minute later with a large slice of apple pie on a tiny saucer. "That's bigger than a normal serving," she said. "Figured you could handle it."

Lance felt the warmth of the woman's kindness and smiled and nodded. "Yes, ma'am. Thank you very much."

He was halfway through his pie—it was fresh, as promised—when he noticed the woman sitting on the stool next to him. He wasn't sure when she'd arrived, but she was there now and looking directly at him.

"I used to put more cinnamon in it," she said. "I don't know why they cut back on it. It was much better that way if you ask me. I think it's too sweet now."

The woman looked much older than Margie, eighty at best but more likely closer to ninety. She wore a plain brown cotton dress and brown leather shoes, stockings visible on the bit of ankle that showed at the hem. Her hair was gray, but still thick, done up in a tight bun atop her head. Her face was so deeply wrinkled it was as if her skin were molding clay, and somebody had dragged the tines of a fork up and down its entire surface.

"I don't think it's too sweet," Lance said, and then turned to see if Margie was in earshot. "But I do think less sugar and more cinnamon would be an improvement."

The woman nodded once. "Of course it would." Then she was quiet for a while, staring ahead toward the kitchen window. Lance stared ahead with her, waiting. She spoke again, this time a little quieter, sadness creeping into her voice. "I don't know why the thing with the pie bothers me so much. They've kept things pretty much the same around here all these years, but the pie ... I was darn near famous for that pie. People used to come from two counties over for *my* pie, and then one day these floozies decide to up and change the recipe. Who do they think they are?"

Lance considered this, took his last bite. "Well," he said, "the folks that remember *your* pie, they're going to know that *this* pie isn't your fault. In fact, if it was as good as you say, those folks are probably just as disappointed as you."

She looked at him and smiled, her teeth were yellowed, but mostly intact. "I suppose you're right, son. I suppose you're right. Guess I never thought of it like that." She pointed an arthritis-gnarled finger at him. "You'd have liked my pie. I know it."

"Yes, ma'am. I believe I would have."

Then they were quiet again. Margie cleared Lance's plate away and he declined more coffee. Hank Peterson paid his tab and left his newspaper when he was finished. The man two stools down took it and flipped to the Sports section. The family with the loud child had left and been replaced by two high-school aged boys who looked sleepy, and Lance wondered why they weren't in class. Through the kitchen window he could see one of the two waitresses counting her tips and joking with one of the unseen cooks.

"So," Lance said, turning to look at the woman on the stool next to him. "How bad is it here?"

The woman closed her eyes, almost as if she were fighting back tears. When she opened them she suddenly looked very tired. "Bad," she said.

Lance nodded. "Yeah ... That's what I was afraid of."

"Are you going to help?"

"I don't know if I can."

"You don't believe that."

Lance placed a twenty on the counter, stood and grabbed his backpack. "No," he said. "But sometimes I wish I did."

He waved goodbye and thanked Margie and then headed for the door. He stopped. On the wall to the left of the door was a photograph in a rough wooden frame, yellowed with age. It was a picture of the woman who'd sat next to him, only in the photograph she was behind the counter and holding a whole pie in her hands and putting on a small grin for the camera. Beneath the photograph was:

Annabelle Winters

1905-1990

Lance turned and looked at the bar stool where she'd been

sitting, now empty. Then he took one last glance at the photo and pushed through the door, out into the world.

DARK GAME IS AVAILABLE NOW

Printed in Great Britain
by Amazon